Madly

Madly

a novel

William Benton

COUNTERPOINT
Berkeley, California

Library of Congress Cataloging-in-Publication Data
Benton, William, 1939-
Madly : a novel / William Benton.
p. cm.
ISBN (10) 1-59376-083-3 (alk. paper)
ISBN (13) 978-1-59376-083-0
I. Title.
PS3552.E59M33 2005
813'.54 — dc22
2005010497

Text design by David Bullen

COUNTERPOINT
2560 Ninth Street, Suite 318
Berkeley, CA 94710
www.counterpointpress.com

Printed in the United States of America

For E.

You reproach yourself for lack of wit
or boldness; but the only way to show
courage would be to love her less.

Stendhal, De l'Amour

Madly

one

I met Irina in late August. I'd gone for a walk and stopped in Blockbuster Video. She stood in the fluorescent brightness at the end of an aisle — tall and stunning with tousled dark hair — examining the cardboard sleeves of several movies. She was dressed in a light aqua-colored windbreaker, jeans and sneakers, a bandanna tied around her forehead. Holding up *Little Vera*, she addressed the employees across the store. "Is this something you would recommend?" Her voice, with a slight accent, maintained a level of formality, a hint of both real and invented distance. They hadn't seen the movie. It was around eleven in the evening, and we were the only customers in the store. "It's not very good," I said. An eloquent delay — a beat — intervened before she acknowledged my presence.

"Well, can you suggest something?" she said, with measured élan.

Jules and Jim was on the shelf in front of her.

"Have you seen this?" I asked.

"No," she said.

"Try it — if you don't like it, I'll give you your money back," I said.

We walked out together. The air was warm, enveloping, scented with fumes of exhaust and the acrid smell of gingko trees. She unlocked her bike.

"I rode twice around park," she said, in a voice that was suddenly bitter, vehement. A tiny mood struck and vanished inexplicably.

"I like to ride at night," she said. "I'm not afraid. So, what do you do?"

"I'm a writer," I said.

"Oh, really. That's what I am," she said. "I just got back from Russia last night. I'm a little tired, but we could meet another time if you want to. I'll give you my number."

A bus glided past, its brightly lit interior empty except for two or three passengers.

"My birthday's coming up in couple of weeks," she said. "Maybe we could meet around then."

We exchanged phone numbers. I studied her face, her elegantly made-up eyes, faultless skin, her teeth present in the penlight of her smile. She carried herself with an air of entitlement, like a model or an actress seen in real life, glasses, a T-shirt wrong-side-out over firm, prominent breasts.

"Does writing always have to be so hard?" she asked.

It was a sincere inquiry, not rhetorical, oddly investing a stranger with the authority to dispense real answers. I mentioned that Pound had once said about writing, "Tell 'em it's fun." She wasn't sure who Pound was, but the statement, with its glittering growl, made immediate sense to her. She took it like an object. At two that morning my phone rang. The machine answered; it was Irina saying how much she liked the movie.

A few days after our first meeting, she called and invited me to brunch at Isabella's, on Columbus Avenue. Her voice had the sound of stage dialogue — of speech hedged in an awkward, fictional elegance.

"We could meet around twelve, if you like — or one, or two."

She arrived dressed in a gray summer suit. Her skirt was long and tight on her hips. We sat outside under the green awning. When the waiter appeared, Irina ordered wine. A careful ritual, barefoot on innocent sand.

"What kind of wine do you have? Do you have anything light — you know, light?" she asked.

He recited a list of wines.

"What do you recommend?"

"The Pinot Grigio," he said.

"Is that light? Well, perhaps I'll try that."

It was like listening to June Christy sing "Something Cool."

While we ate she was a little nervous and at one point knocked a fork off the table. It allowed me to say something or other that dissolved the tension. The act became, for a moment, the chime of a minor intimacy. The sun was coming under the awning. We'd taken a step toward each other. It happened again — if not that day, soon after — and turned into a fetish of hers. The fork falling to the floor — and the sunny grace that rushed to envelop her. A year later, walking past Isabella's late one night, I think we both saw it at the same time: on the sidewalk, near where we'd sat that first day, lay a fork. Irina picked it up — and then threw it away, its tinny metal ringing on the pavement.

After brunch we strolled down to Riverside Park. Sunbathers lay in the grass on counterpanes and beach towels, women with bare backs reading the *Times*, their undone tops lying lifelessly in place beneath white, blue-veined breasts. We sat on the promenade at the edge of the river. Nearby, a man was fishing for eels.

"Well . . . if you wouldn't mind," she said, "I could show you some of my poetry. I have it with me."

Her face glowed with delicate expectancy, held in check by a practiced composure. The corners of her mouth turned up, like a detail in a Leonardo drawing — not a smile, but a permanent muscular complement. As she handed me the poems she was talking in several directions at once, saying that she wrote poetry in Russian and in English, that she wasn't sure what she was doing, that she'd also tried to write a novel in English, and that in Europe life was different, that men supported women there, but that here you had to make a living. Her hand floated up and fluttered around her collar. "I have on this blouse — it's *lavender*," she said, out of nowhere. "Maybe I can sometime show you novel. You have to pay, in one way or another, that's how it works in this country." Her speech, including its occasional dislocutions, moved in formal cadences. As she spoke she smiled at you, like a stranger imparting sad news.

The Hudson, wide and calm, flowed upstream with the incoming tide. You could smell the sea, a faint mineral cleanness. In the hurrying current, a submerged timber drifted by. Beyond the silhouette of her face, in bright haze, the masts at the Seventy-ninth Street Boat Basin stood still against the sky. Gulls trolled the glitter.

"Read this one first," she urged, pulling it out of the stack. "Then the one under it." Seated beside me, she continued to talk in a slightly disconnected way about herself; her long legs, bare and muscular, were crossed within the narrow confines of her skirt.

I read through all her poems. They were strangely unclear, but impressive, filled with striking, surrealist images. I asked her which poets she liked, whom she was reading. She said she didn't read very much. "That's one of my problems. I'm not too good staying home and reading." Her voice took on an odd, clinical tone. "It's called a quick fix — you know, a quick fix? It's usually sex. Sometimes with men, sometimes with women. It doesn't matter — what's the big deal?" She wasn't coming on to me; it was a kind of batty candor, unsettling, but weirdly touching. A person began to emerge, like a figure in a cubist portrait. She'd been in America for six years. Her mother used to walk around their Moscow apartment naked, taking an "air bath." For a while she had been a coat-check girl in an Upper East Side restaurant, and then worked as an exotic dancer making fifteen hundred dollars a night. She was twenty-five. She'd been married three times.

On the back of a card, the night we met, she'd written her name and phone number. In quickly formed printed letters it read "Irina Pieropova." Then, one afternoon, introduced to someone, she said her name was Irina *Mirokova*. She'd also told me that her real name was Elvira, but that she hated the way Americans pronounced it, as well as its witchy association in pop culture, and had chosen Irina instead.

"What about 'Mirokova' and 'Pieropova'?" I asked. "Is one a married name?"

"No. I'm just thinking of changing it," she said.

"Which one should I use if I write you a letter?"

She was casually equivocal.

"Pieropova, I think. Or Mirokova — which do you like?"

"I don't know. What's your real name?" I asked.

"Mirokova."

"Is that the name you grew up with?"

"Yes."

"Well, why not use that one?"

"O.K., Mirokova — but with one *r*," she stipulated.

"How was it spelled in Russia?" I asked.

"With one *r*."

She was from Moscow. Her father was a high school gymnastics coach and held an appointed, administrative position. Her mother taught French cooking in the same school. "My father is tall — like you, only not so skinny. He is always calm. He was invited to the Summer Olympics in Australia. He never raises voice. But Mother is French — you know, half-French? They were hippies — I guess you'd say — when they were young."

Mauve eye shadow, which announced the depth of her eyes, was blended in a silver tone out to the strong ridge of her brow.

"Then I lived with Grandmother. My father came once a year to visit me — you *know*?" This is said in a way that assumes I share a sympathetic knowledge of what has happened.

"Why was that?" I asked.

"What?"

"Why were you separated from your parents?"

"Oh. It's long story. I'll tell you sometime."

Details of her life were revealed obliquely, not, it seemed, with an intention on her part to mask or withhold things, but more as a kind of failure to locate and control their context in her mind.

For twelve years, starting in her early childhood, she studied violin and piano. She had an older brother. When she was sixteen she attended the Moscow Textile Institute and lived in a dorm. "My father was against it, but I talked him into letting me. One of my roommates was wild girl. She was very pretty. Guys came every night. She loved to do it — that's all. She didn't care. I wasn't interested in sex. There would be all these boys, drinking and hanging around. And the problem was, her name was Elvira, same as mine. So they would think I was her."

By the time she was seventeen she was the mistress of one of the heads of the Russian Mafia. "I had my own apartment, drove Mercedes, and carried around cash in bags. I could have anything I wanted — while rest of city was fighting in streets for piece of bread."

"How did you manage to meet this Mafia person?" I asked.

"He wasn't the first one. There were others before that."

His name was Konstantin; he was fifty. "Of course I had to take younger lover — an actor. It was very dangerous. Konstantin would have killed him if he found out — and me too." There was a trip to Sweden involving another wealthy older man ("They all square and hairy") who owned a chain of exclusive shops. "I was supposed to work for him. He put me up in fancy hotel, bought me presents, even a Cartier watch, you know, real." Her ability to orchestrate the cross-purposes of men, to dance in and out of the fire with fearless disdain, was her passport. She discovered it and her beauty in the same mirror; shame she already knew.

"I never slept with shop owner. He was demanding me to do it all the time, but I made excuses, you know, blamed my period." She laughs effervescently, brimming with the tale she is telling. "Then one day he cornered me and said that either I become his mistress or return all the money and presents. I talked him into taking me away to spa in the country. I promised we would spend all week together, making love."

She eluded him. At one of the stops she stepped off the train and onto another, bound in the opposite direction. He thought she was in the restroom. She never saw him again. Whole parts of her life, involving real risk, were made up of postures — the capework of movie star derring-do — performed under the watchful eyes of angels.

It's a brilliant winter day. Gulls wheel high over the reservoir in Central Park. I haven't seen or spoken to her in months. For a moment suspended — suffused — the flute-notes of who she was run into the room.

Her first marriage took place in Sweden when she was eighteen. She met him there. Perhaps he was from Switzerland. She said only that after a while he was quiet and moody. She dismissed it all. "We were same age, we thought we were in *love*." A little later, in the mechanical tone of something learned by rote, she said, "When you are obsessed it means you want something you can't have." She added, "I did that once." She returned to Moscow, to Konstantin. She didn't marry Konstantin — he was already married and had a family. Instead, he arranged for a friend of his to marry Irina as an expedient to obtain a visa for her. It was purely business. As a married woman, Irina could travel. The three of them came to Washington, where Konstantin was negotiating a deal with Lockheed Aircraft. She had touched it — America — felt its obsidian glance pass over her. She talked Konstantin into letting her stay and attend business school in New York, ostensibly to be of benefit to his operations. "I knew I was not going back; I tricked him." Her life is a series of leaps from stepping-stone to stepping-stone — or, in her perception of it, a series of dramatic escapes. It is the normal mode of her progress on the earth. Various forces conspire to oppose its momentum. Love is one of these.

She quit business school and went to work as a coat-check girl in a French restaurant on the Upper East Side, encountering in her first American job the poor pay, long hours, and empty routine of menial employment. The smell of wealth and wet snow, sable against her face, she lugged the heavy furs up and down a narrow stairway. She skated to work on roller blades through Central Park. She dated a biker. One day a young man and his mother, a famous fashion designer, came in for lunch. He was beautiful. They returned the next day, and the next. Finally he spoke to Irina, told her he was in love with her. This is America, you fly on fairy wings. She showed me a photograph taken of them at the Rainbow Room. They looked surprisingly alike, drinking champagne, stars and glitter scattered on the table in front of them. Within weeks they were married and had moved to Barcelona. Eight months later, in a villa in St. Thomas, she caught him with a homosexual lover.

Midnight in New York.

"I got my same job again," she said. "Everybody is very happy to see me. The cook gave me caviar pies. Then one night, that week or maybe next — very soon after I got back — one of regular customers asked me if I wanted to go into show business. You know — they call it show business. He told me what it was — dancing at club. I was interested, so he drove me — I don't know where it was — Bronx or Queens. Somewhere out of town. There was woman who helped new girls. How to put on makeup and what costume to wear. It was very safe. They don't let anybody touch you. That's rule! No one can touch. If they do, they get thrown out of club. Anyway, I made seven hundred dollars in three hours. Then limo guy to bring you back. After while, I was transferred to club in Manhattan. I was very good — you know! Some nights I made more than two thousand dollars. You didn't have to go out with them unless you wanted to. I would always let them think I was going. I hated them! You know what it's like in these clubs."

"I've never been to one," I said.

"Oh, come on!" she said.

"It's true, I haven't."

"I don't believe you."

"Still, it's true."

"Well . . . anyway. Where was I?" she asked.

"You hated the men in the clubs," I said.

"I *despised* them! I could kill them right now!"

Her lips peeled back from her teeth.

"What about your marriage — what happened?"

"We got divorce," she shrugged. "I didn't ask for anything. All my friends said I was crazy. But I didn't want his money. I was making so much, I didn't need it by then."

Place on these events an overlay, a scribbled map of missing distances and distorted definition. Her life is a state of deflected meaning — moods fractured at the speed of light, visions vivid as movies, a din of voices in her brain, black flares of paranoia. She is confused and confusing. Her mother told her, "When you were a little girl, someone must have dropped you on your head."

It isn't that facts have to be assembled or dramatized, but that truths have to be faced. Not plot, but destiny. When I say I don't know what will happen, that doesn't change the face of the ground. From still points, glances land and test the boundaries — or fly through, their smiles left like posters on the walls. The suddenly raised volume, a door pushed open onto the snowy street. Accept that.

She had her hair cut sometimes as often as once a week. "He's a gay," she explained. "They crazy, you know how they are, but he likes me. Normally it's three hundred and fifty, but I get discount." Jagged, pixie-length, it ranged in color from umber to "mahogany" to auburn. Her face was heart-shaped with wide cheekbones, dark arched eyebrows like bird wings. It was a Slavic face, modulated by Persian antecedents. "My grandmother was Islamic." Her eyes were large and black, enhanced by a mild strabismus. In unrelenting profile, in the sunlight of somewhere we had gone, her eyes glinted hazel-brown in their turned-away gaze. She had soft ears.

I saw her almost every day for months before I saw the same dress twice. Many things were no doubt acquired during her marriage to the celebrated designer's son. Others were purchased with the cash she got from exotic dancing — money transformed into glorious and vindictive lingerie. Recently, at the Guggenheim, I saw an exhibition of Armani designs. A vast parade of exquisite attire filled the museum. It looked like Irina's wardrobe. The various dresses and gowns were supported by concealed forms, like costumes on ghosts — or like intimate images of her absence. I stopped in front of a black, floor-length lace gown, recognizing the stance. Her weight rests on one leg, shoulders back and down, hips thrust slightly forward. One arm dangles behind her body, the other is poised in front of her, like loose ribbons of a bow you could pull to unwrap it all.

A few days after our brunch, we went to the Broadway show *Fosse*. We met at the theater, outside on the crowded sidewalk. Irina wore a thin, plum-colored dress, with a see-through veil window in its bodice. Her breasts were clearly visible, bra-less, their nipples unanticipated. What separates you from this is not the convention of fabric but an imperial decision, it seemed to say. A light wrap could with insouciance be drawn together. Her body resembled the dancers onstage, leggy and athletic. In the lobby after the play, she stopped to try on a *Fosse* baseball cap. "Can I have one of these?" The main song from the show, "Life Is Just a Bowl of Cherries," contained a phrase we appropriated for a while.

> The sweet things in life
> to you were just loaned,
> so how can you lose
> what you've never owned?

We got a taxi in the rain — a rare, huge, unburdening rain, like something in the tropics. In my apartment we watched the lightning splinter across the sky. We were lying on the couch, kissing. I had pulled her down on top of me. She asked about lightning, how it worked.

"You really don't know?"

"Well, not exactly. Tell me," she said.

In words spoken between kisses I explained lightning. Her face was still slightly cool from the rain.

"I wonder which one of us is positive and which one is negative," she said. It changed in midair from a real question to a flirtatious remark. A pensive note, caught, and turned lightly into familiar music.

"Do you want to go to bed?" I asked.

"I like having my breath stop," she said.

I fit a pattern in Irina's life. Although I didn't have money, I had something she wanted. I'd published a number of books of poetry. I wasn't famous, but I was — difficult perhaps to stumble across in the circles she traveled in — a "real" poet. Like most poets, I was prepared to believe that talent could come unsuspected from anywhere. The apparent disorder in Irina's thinking wasn't something that warned me off; if anything, it fit into the bias of my life, its risks and deficits. I took her seriously as a writer. Her mind ran away with itself, the way it does in dreams, foundering on a surfeit of associations. Yet it was something she lived with. "Did I stop making sense?" Her imperfections created an allowance for my own. We were poets. We could meet like warriors after the fact.

On her twenty-sixth birthday, she said, "Now, when is yours?"

"October."

"Next month! So, how old will you be?"

I was suddenly aware of how much I wanted what had begun between us to continue.

"A hundred," I said.

"No, come on, tell me," she urged.

"Forty-nine," I said, reluctantly.

"Forty-nine," she repeated, lifting an eyebrow. "You look lot younger. I thought you like thirty-seven."

"I wish I were."

"Why? You great! It's probably from running. Or drinking beer," she added, laughing.

"It doesn't bother you?"

"Nyet. I always go with older men — even more than you. I don't like guys my own age. They too stupid."

Her face was luminous, her bare youthful arms. But present in the enormous attraction, like a gratuitous condition in its breadth, was the appeal that it was exactly our disparities and limitations that might prove transcendent.

There was something else that had, in a sad and inadvertent way, a bearing on our being together. I met Irina at almost the same time that my ex-wife, from whom I'd been divorced for several years, died of cancer. We had been close friends. We had dinner together two or three times a month and spoke regularly on the phone. She had striking, wide-apart eyes, slightly down-turned, in an angular face that was quick to laugh. Gilot on the beach at Antibes. For all its troubled and difficult times, our marriage remained — in the tag-code of memory — a bright, hieratic image. I saw her last when she was preparing to go to an experimental clinic in Baja California. She looked thinner than I remembered, but radiant, young. We went over a list of things she wanted me to take care of if she died — housekeeping details (there was no money, no estate), what to give to whom, concerns about pets. It was a conversation without morbidity or the slightest emotional wavering. She made jokes to relieve my clumsiness. Afterwards, we went for a walk near her apartment in Brooklyn Heights and talked about our daughter, who was in college. She suggested that we stop by and look at the first ornamental plums that had begun to blossom in a neighborhood park. It was a cold March day. On the way, she needed to rest, and we sat on the low wall of a brownstone in a shaft of sunlight that fell between two tall buildings in the near distance. She held my arm and leaned her head into my shoulder. Nothing of any emotional consequence was said. Our speech continued with its own random pace and connections. Its ordinariness was the source of its luminescence, its living, enlaced duration. In the park the dense white blossoms on the trees looked like popcorn that had suddenly exploded. "Walt Whitman Plaza," she said. "It's too cold to stay, I just wanted you to see it. I like sitting here." Back at her apartment, when I got ready to leave, I held her and told her I loved her. She walked me out to the landing and we waved good-bye. As I started down the stairs she smiled and said, "We had a great life." By the time I reached the street, wondering if I had ever loved anyone else, I was in tears.

My ex-wife had come to New York from Canada to study photography when she was eighteen. She worked as a waitress in the Village and met a man in his late thirties, a dashing, Jewish, would-be writer who had lived in Paris. They married and had a son. Her husband, it developed, was a junkie who used to send her out "to score" from street dealers while she was pregnant. A year or so later, he killed himself with an overdose of heroin, leaving a note, spattered with threads of red, that blamed her. We met the following year, through a mutual friend who had been her lover. We were both in our early twenties and answered for each other the first tentative purchase on an adult life. She was Flemish-looking, witty, slender, clear-hearted. Her name was Irene.

Russell Hoban writes somewhere, "Everything is a coincidence, we just miss most of them." And of course the obverse is equally true, that there is no such thing as a coincidence. Each event has its own weight and import and is only trivialized by the idea of empty synchronicities. Yet it was also impossible to ignore the fact that the death of Irene was accompanied almost to the day by the advent in my life of Irina. I refused to make anything out of it. The timing of events and their names I knew meant nothing, yet they remained an evocative presence in my mind, a form of innocuous persuasion that dovetailed with my will to, say, underwrite the inexplicable lack of sense that turned up in Irina's speech — which I was then first encountering — or to soften the aura by which this beautiful Russian poet had made herself a part of my life.

Daniel, Irene's son, was four and a half when we moved from New York to Oregon, where I had been offered a teaching job. We'd been married for a little over two years and had by now an infant daughter of our own. On a winding road in the mountains, as we were driving back to Portland from the coast, a lone pickup truck came toward us in our lane suddenly from around a blind curve. There was no shoulder on our right; a vertical wall of rock rose up from almost the edge of the pavement. The other side of the road was a sheer drop-off. At the last second, to avoid a head-on collision, I swerved into the opposite lane. There was no other traffic on the road. The driver of the truck, as it turned out, was drunk and must have only at the last instant become aware of us. He tried to pull back into his own lane, and the truck's front fender hit the rear end of our car. The impact caused us to skid violently off the road into the gravel, and the car blew a tire. It turned over twice; I assumed we had begun to tumble down the cliff and waited for the world to go black.

The car came to a stop, right side up in the middle of the road. My one thought, frantic in its intensity, was to find out if Irene was all right. When it was clear that she was not hurt, everything else shifted to another level. The world came back into focus, sunlight on the road, the silence, a vast desolate burn of timber on a mountainside in the distance. A couple from Portland, who were traveling to the coast, drove us to the hospital. Both children had suffered head injuries and were unconscious. Halfway to the hospital, our daughter began to cry. Daniel was dead when I carried him into the emergency room.

My wife's struggle to come to terms with the loss of her son took place over a long time. It was accomplished not so much by the process of acceptance as by a blind permeation. Certain of her qualities were heightened, others eliminated. Absurdity, rather than wit, became the substance of her humor. A subtlety of mind was replaced by scarcely more than a cursory, incurious attention concerning anything that was intellectually or emotionally demanding. Pain centers were guarded by a seismic threshold, and pleasure, its evil twin, was forbidden. She couldn't make love to me. All the kisses and tender interplay that exist between lovers came to an end. In rare instances, after months of abstinence, Irene herself would sometimes initiate sex. But it was only the base act — perfunctory, voracious, biological — without gossamer affection. I waited two years, until it was obvious that this had become the reality of our lives, and then — with more or less Irene's blessing — began an affair with a student of mine.

Much of a marriage remains invisible, the hard metals melted down in private. I couldn't leave her. I came close at one point, a year or so later. I was romantic and wanted the woman whose passion I shared to be the woman in my life. The decision to stay carried with it an unspoken, and in part unexamined, corollary: if I were going to have an intimate relationship with anyone, it would be at the expense of discounting their importance in my life. It became an irrevocable part of my character, and the bond with my wife took on a strength that reflected its exemption from romantic dependence; it was unassailable. Years later, when we did finally separate, it was she who left. She went back to Canada alone and lived with her mother for the next two or three years, and then returned to New York, where her life had been, where we were.

The women I was subsequently with continued to have — in the gravitational field of my marriage — the status of mistresses. Even in the few cases where new love and the possibility of a life together with someone were at stake, I couldn't quite extricate myself from the past. While Irene and I were married, my attitude toward the women who were my lovers had, in the context of our lives, the default of virtue. The same attitude toward women, now that I was free, was unfounded, shallow. It disturbed me, yet I couldn't stop it.

It was not until I met Irina that things changed. (*Irene, Irina* — the river of their syllables whispers each other; women connected not by metaphysical design, but by love and chance, like paired numbers in a throw of the dice.) Irina's mental problems conveyed to anyone with whom she was involved the immediate advantage they possessed over her. She was hit on persistently by "photographers" whom she'd take seriously and then, lured to their studios, be hurt and angry when it turned out they were only trying to get her into bed. The fact that we were both poets provided a way to dissolve advantage and establish a ground upon which we could not meet *except* as equals. As I got to know her better this became one of the arguments I repeatedly invoked against the attempts Irina made to deny her own worth. Because it was an active principle in our lives, or because I realized that by being a poet I was uniquely qualified to pronounce upon its truth, or because I could help her and felt the tide-pull of being needed — however it came about, I not only loved her as an equal, I felt, for the first time in years, elevated to the position.

I grew up in a small Texas town on Galveston Bay, the only male in a houseful of women — my grandmother, my great-grandmother, a crazy aunt, and my mother. They moved like light on water through my life. I was spoiled, uncontrollable. When I was four I wrote letters to my father, lies to charm him out of the sky. He was a fighter-pilot, a handsome, alien presence in the photographs my mother showed me. They divorced when I was a year old. In a household managed by my grandmother with patrician care, my mother was like a beautiful older sister to me, young, blue-eyed with exotic black hair; I was doted upon, treated like a collaborator. She taught ballroom dancing at Arthur Murray's Studio, and by the time I was seven I knew how to samba, waltz, tango, and jitterbug. We played records late into the night and danced, I and this glamorous, adoring conspirator in my upbringing. I knew dozens and dozens of love songs by heart, which I sang in a seven-year-old's Sinatra voice, longing and heroic loss — "For you I cry, for you dear only" — the fictions I slipped into like an oversized raincoat. Girls in my neighborhood and at elementary school, their hair bouncing as they ran, evoked in me huge wedges of emotion. I not only wanted them; they were essential in the landscape of my imagination. I had been designed in their pursuit.

From more or less this height, I watched the descent of my mother in the town's three or four bars. I played the jukebox — friend of my youth — with its eternal theme that only the star-crossed, the devoured know love at all, framed in rainbow bubbles. But my life, as the child of an alcoholic, was filled with scenes, betrayal, and havoc. As I got older I fought against what seemed to me a travesty of love's honor. My mother's deceits and disregard, her weaseling attempts to twist things, to sacrifice the truth of her child's perceptions rather than admit wrong, sharpened the pains of my logic, the edges of my rage. Our battles became, for my mother, the primary intimacy that we shared. Bitter, orchestrated displays of intensity took the place of bonds based on more condign emotions. With a sense of guilt that found its only satisfaction in the punishment her son could dispense, she would come home drunk and start fights that left us both in emotional shambles. I could be counted on to show disgust, invoke envenomed silences. Or to holler at her, call her a drunk and a whore. These were, to the extent that I felt and acted upon them, my own emotions. But they were also part of a dance — as much as any other I had learned from her. If I tried to leave the room, she would stop me or follow me into another part of the house. Once, when she stood blocking the door to the kitchen, I tried to move her out of the way. The second I touched her arm, she threw herself backwards onto the floor. "How dare you attack me!" she bellowed. Even in the middle of these performances I was aware of the farce, the logical slippage that held it together, aware that this in lieu of any other was our communion.

My aunt, her sister, a quaint and pale apparition in the garden, had mental problems. "Do you know the real name of these flowers, Bill? They're called When-You-Bend." But my grandmother, strain mitered into the fineness of her features, reminded me that she was ill. The madness of my mother's life was explained by sighs, by silences. Men came in the middle of the night threatening to break down the doors — "Eve, you rotten bitch!" On my bike I'd sometimes see her rusted, maroon convertible in the parking lot of a motel, the sun bleaching its red leather seats. Yet our lives were, however dysfunctional, unforsaken. Like any mother, she was the woman I adored. I possessed but could not keep her.

In front of the house where I lived was a long, dilapidated pier, a vestige of displaced prosperity, like the big screened-in porch furnished with rusty gliders and lounge chairs, the breezeway

connecting the back of the house to the kitchen, giant mag-
nolias in the yard. When it was first built, sometime in the
twenties, the pier had been a slender, wooden aisle extending
out over the water to a length of 1,200 feet. A couple could
stroll on it arm in arm. Over the years it had been decimated
by hurricanes and neglect. As a very young child, when my
grandmother bought the house, I remember its dark stumps
receding in symmetrical pairs, absent their cross-members
and planking, out and out into the gray water. We didn't have
the money to restore the pier, but with the help of kids in the
neighborhood, it was kept in a haphazard but functional state.
The pilings were sound, covered up to the high-water mark
with stockings of sharp barnacles. Near the shore, where my
grandmother and aunt would sometimes set out crab lines, it
was kept wide enough for them to move safely around on, in
their straw hats and summer dresses. But beyond that point, the
rest of the pier narrowed to a patchwork of long, single boards,
placed lengthwise one after the other in a staggered, arbitrary
pattern, where no one else in my family would venture.

I could see the pier from my upstairs room, a jagged crack
splitting the wide tattery shine of moonlight. I fished from it,
swam from it, relished its freedom and isolation. At its end,
where the boathouse used to be, with its slip and hoist for the
sleek, mahogany runabouts with plush leather seats that could
still be seen on the Bay — small flags waving from the stern,
above the baritone of their inboards — was now a desolate
stand of pilings, some rising up to the height of a rooftop, others broken off midway or ominously submerged. The air was
filled with the wilder smell of deep water, and waves shook the
pier — or on calm days the thick backs of alligator gars broke
the surface with the diamond-shaped scales of their hide, like
the tread of a tire. At its end, one was too far from the shore to
be recognized and beyond the range of a voice.

Day after day I sprinted full speed, like a broken field runner, racing dizzily the length of the pier, faster and faster, over the narrow boards as they danced back and forth in their erratic placement beneath my feet. When I veer off into the air, shattering the water with a slicing, sideways dive, the change of element transforms me into an eleven-year-old boy, surfacing in the sun. But the runner on the pier keeps pace with my life. It's a persisting portrait of myself, the image of exposed longing, ithyphallic, bound up in the trajectory of impasse. Toward an exquisite, unreachable limit, without audience or competitor, I ran breathing evanescent glory, aware of the fall that would come, the sudden slip on an algae-green, wave-sloshed plank. From the calm center of my exertion, I watched the water's burnished surface, the negative grid in the glittering points of brilliance.

My life I'm sure was to a great extent shaped by the sense of inadequacy I learned at eleven or twelve. It was another layer, added to the absence of a father, but more emphatic, wilder in its need; the compensations that grew out of it were more desperate and self-involved. Love becomes a deity of doubtful existence that you throw yourself into the arms of — the sexual act its sacrament. I was fifteen when I left home. The secret agonies of my mother's life were beyond the reach of my character. A habit of mind formed that registered betrayal with seismic sensitivity, setting off the hair triggers of a vehement defense system — boyish and strangely empty, a simple consuming reflex, a war whoop.

At sixteen, thin and tall, I wore dark suits and smoked Camels. I was a fake adult, a barroom piano player, a poet impostor. I sang love songs to the waitresses and single women who sat with their legs crossed sipping tall drinks served with flamingo stirs. We walked out to their cars in the salt night air. My mother would turn up in the clubs where I worked, with one of her boyfriends, and wave merrily from the dance floor, or ask me to play a song. With her hazy noir blessing, I was fulfilling the life she'd prepared me for. I lived in a motel, worked until three or four in the morning, and read books during the day. I left Texas with a band and spent the winter in Miami, where I stayed after the band broke up, playing in a hotel on the beach as a single. The *Miami Herald* did a lead feature on me; I remained in Florida, appearing as a singer-pianist in cocktail lounges of the big hotels, bored with the repetition, the years. An autodidact lacks the means to measure himself. I felt the weight of my stupidities, their awkward scraping against the workings of the world. My life was formed by fumes, dreams, women. A book of my poems was published, I moved to New York, married. I wrote other books, taught at colleges. My daughter grew up. In the apartment, where I lived alone, I worked at my desk through the evening hours, the summer scent of decomposing leaves floating up from the park, and then went out for a walk in the humid August night.

It would be purely fanciful to attempt to line up the meridians of my life with Irina's. We backlit the inwound histories of each other. Dots moved across an uncharted present, toward the vector of their encounter.

"O rus! / *Horace* / O Rus!" Pushkin wrote in *Eugene Onegin*. I carried Russia in my middle name.

New York is an altar for couples of unlikely provenance. You see them every day. They are a part of the impersonal, anonymous aspect of the city, which in turn becomes the mist they awaken in. It is their otherwise unremarkable lives, made visible by the aura of alliance, that is perceived — and envied. Love itself reveals them. They are no different from other couples — they ordain the inherent difference *in* other couples. Their disparity is noted because it is expressed as a form of triumph, where tenderness has prevailed at face value.

Nothing in Irina's life possessed, on its own, a simple clarity; overlapping purposes were the branches she peered through. She was born in Moscow in 1973; to her private instability the world she grew up in added its own. She learned early that life consisted of transactions. To acquire fresh fruit at the market you used adolescent allure like promissory notes. "One time — I was fifteen or sixteen — I end up in worker-guy's apartment. I don't know how I got there. I'd barely had my first man. He took it out. It was *huge*! Poor man. He was from Georgia. They hairy and brown. I was trying to figure out how to get away, he had me pinned down on bed. But he couldn't get it — you know — in. I was moving like a snake, so he couldn't do it. He got mad at me and lost erection. So then, I pretend to be willing. I go to bathroom, moving very slow, caressing his shoulder." Her voice deepens to a mischievous timbre. "I was beguiling — you know, beguiling? Then in bathroom I got dressed and ran down the stairs. He is naked in the bed so couldn't catch me. I was scared to death."

We became a part of each other's lives; it happened more or less the way it always does. The instant I say that, I'm aware it's not true. It is a wish — a lapse — a boast that our lives share with others an equal weight. It is also, curiously, the will to discount something as a cliché purely to possess it, to be behind its closed door with Irina — for all the world to see.

There had been a point at the very beginning, the day we sat on the promenade and I read her poetry, when I knew, like something decided in the sky, that she was available to me. It wasn't arrogance or even the result of a design on my part; it was both more arbitrary and more miraculous. The frisson of knowing it — the sudden tendril of awareness — existed in the fact that it had been communicated not by anything she expressed directly, but as an adjunct to everything she had said. Nothing flirtatious had occurred between us. It was an eventuality, without prelude and without indefiniteness. A pure sexual connection — preserving all the distances that are normally dissolved in increments of ritual and seduction — was brought into stunning immediacy in the exquisite face and body of a stranger.

After we had been together for several weeks, I began to miss the evolving intimacy that naturally forms between lovers. We seemed to start over from day to day, as if a part of the process had been inexplicably suspended. The distance and reserve with which she conducted herself, by remaining unchanged, had grown conspicuous, weird.

"I think we should begin to think of ourselves as being together," I said.

She sat on the edge of the couch with her legs stretched out in front of her, wide apart.

"Being together," she repeated. She pursed her lips in a tight smile and made her chin long, her mouth full of air.

"O.K., let's be together," she said.

One's losses, past, one's empty bed are a part of the beginning. She is gorgeous. She writes poems about us. It's too compelling to second-guess, too drenched in its own rush, her ribs against my mouth, the side of her breast, the earth far beneath us. At this stage the idea of something amiss in her brain only contributes to a sense of abandon, like the impunity of masked lovers.

If, for her, advantage was a seamless component of desire, then desire itself was, conceivably, purer for it. There are always jagged edges. She called me every day; it became a habit between us, rather than me calling her. I was perhaps the less interested one at first, cautious of this curiously troubled girl. And also, whenever I did call, the voice that answered was cold, somnambulistic, tortured, alone. A wall of rejection. It was always an effort to kick-start it, to bring her voice into the light of simple words and feelings. When she called me, the emotional preparation had taken place, the melody of want was in it. I loved the mildly schizophrenic construction of her greeting: "Hello, Bill — that's me."

Hemingway wrote that he knew Zelda Fitzgerald was insane when she said to him, "Ernest, don't you think Al Jolson is greater than Jesus?" One night Irina made a remark that reminded me of this. She was relaxed, the facade of her defenses down. We'd just made love. It was almost always true: at three in the morning, candles burning, her hair wet from the shower, she was clear and present. I'd fix scrambled eggs that she'd eat in bed and then sleep, "seeing dreams," till noon. There had been, from the beginning, certain things I'd noticed. In conversation she related everything to herself in that excessive way that's blind to its own awkward behavior. When she talked — she loved to talk — an almost desperate energy would sometimes take over, a manic animation, in which her thoughts ran together, their connections falling away. But she was foreign, insecure, and these qualities were, at least on one level, an attempt to be forthcoming. On this occasion, she produced a secret, a confidence. She'd seen a vision in which Jesus Christ appeared to her. "Do you know what color the sun really is? It's blue. The other side of the sun is *blue*! He showed me this." What does one say? "Please don't be crazy," I whispered. My voice was weak, incantatory. "Be beautiful and talented, but please don't be crazy."

A night or two after this, we were on the couch listening to music. She was lying in my arms.

"Do you know this song?"

"I don't believe so," she said.

"I think it's Rachmaninoff."

"Well, then I probably know," she said.

As the singer's voice began its ravishing descent, I kissed her. Her lips were unresponsive, her teeth clenched shut.

"What's wrong?" I asked.

She didn't answer.

I tried to kiss her again. Suddenly she stood up, shouting, "Don't touch me! I can't stand for you to touch me!" It was frightening and inexplicable. I didn't know what to say or do. In the stunned silence, she put on her shoes and left.

At midnight the following evening, she showed up at my apartment.

"What am I doing, dragging you out of bed?" she said. "Come on, let's go have drink — it's early."

"I don't know if I want to have a drink with you," I said.

"Come on, please!" She grabbed my arm, pulling weakly on it in a girlish gesture. "I'm sorry about last night."

"You know, that's what prostitutes do — you can sleep with them, but you can't kiss them."

"I'm not a prostitute," she said. "It was PMS — you know, PMS? I have bad sometimes."

In her fabulous dress, her perfect face, she struck a pose, a semaphore of petulance.

"Please," she said, "just one drink."

We walked over to a bar on Broadway. A guitar player, bearded and fat, wearing a tropical shirt, was playing "Little Girl Blue" in rich jazz chords.

"If I hurt you, I don't want to," she said. "I just do things sometimes."

When the waitress came, Irina said, "Bring him beer, he needs two beers!"

I reached over and touched her face, her hair.

"I used to be worse!" she said.

"What do you mean?"

"It was form of recreation, almost."

"What?"

"Well, I would seek men out maliciously," she said.

"What did you do?"

"You know — go with them. To their apartments — anywhere. They so sure — is what I let them think. They get to the highest pitch of anticipation — you know? — and then, abruptly — I walk away." Her face is a mask of relived anger as she tells me this. She is there, an evil satisfaction burning in her eyes.

This is not for an instant a catalog of aberrations. It's the rustle of knives, the glint of moonlight on the surrounding foliage. Her flaws were daffy, vivid, like the missing noses on statues of Aphrodite. She arrived carrying flowers and suddenly dissolved in a blur of paranoia. "I knew it was a mistake the minute I walked in here tonight. I shouldn't have come." These qualities, stained bright by irrationality, were not only separable from an essential center, they assisted in revealing it. The lilt of her soul came through. Elusive, eclipsed by the gaudy banality of mental disturbance, it was still a case, as Stevens writes, for the lover to ask, "Whose spirit is this?" The same was true of her looks, of how beautiful she really was once you got past the empty fictions of fashion and glamour. Her unmade-up face was prettiest, not because of the virtues of "a natural look," but because she was less constrained, less reliant upon an intended impact. In just the shift from glasses to contacts her face mobilized itself toward a singular objective. Murder crept into her eyes.

A lot of her confusion floated here, like Ophelia's gauzy gown. All the successes of her life had so far depended entirely on her ability to seduce. In every transaction her looks, her sexual leverage was the sole value she possessed. Fashion, airs, pretensions turned on a risky pivot; it was a substitute life, not a real one. Yet it was *image*; the sun was blue. Fake life is a sanctuary, precisely because reality is elsewhere. The mechanism itself served inner forces, vaguely glimpsed in the satisfaction of pain inflicted, of icy, emotional immunity. Love could be sneered at and self-worth perverted in the pure artful execution of her life. We broke up once, after being together for several months. While we were apart, she slept with someone else. When we got back together she said with inverted pride, "You have no idea how much my heart was not touched."

There is a passage in Pasternak's autobiographical book *Safe Conduct* where he develops an idea about art that takes as its starting point a boy's sexual imagination. Pasternak writes four pages of decorously unspecific prose, charting out to a logical end a system of causes that evolves, through an inherent respect for women, into the existence of art itself.

> The movement which gives rise to a beginning is the cleanest of all things known to the universe. And with this cleanness alone which has conquered so often through the ages it would be enough that by contrast everything else which is not it should smack of profound earthiness.
>
> And there is art. It is concerned not with man but with the image of man. The image of man, as becomes apparent, is greater than man.

Irina's life was the upside down of this, of the inchoate conditions of sex as the cleanest of all things. But there was art. She was an image-maker. We went one night to Lincoln Center to hear Mahler's *Resurrection*, and when we left the concert Irina, enthralled, began to tell me about it.

"There was an angel and below the angel they were shooting arrows. The red arrows were evil and the gold arrows good. The angel let the gold arrows pass into the world, but he caught all the evil arrows, stopping them."

"Where did you see this?" I asked.

"In there! I saw him do it. He reached out and caught them in midair! He was very fast."

For a while she was so sure of the vision she couldn't quite understand that I hadn't seen it also. In moments like this, it was hard to find the exact footing to talk to her. Madness wears a cloak of invincibility. I felt her slipping away and was helpless to prevent it. Around us, crowds of people were crossing the plaza. A dozen couples sat on the black marble apron of the fountain, which sent its brightly lit plinth of water into the air. I took her hand, which was lifeless, in both of mine. I don't remember what I said — nothing, hollow lost words, blindly feeling for her in the dark. She took her hand away.

Irina knew she had problems and most of the time wasn't defensive about them. As a matter of fact, her problems were her mythos, the source of an epic self-involvement. "I hope I'm not split," she said when she first began to tell me about herself. She thought of her visions as occult phenomena or some kind of augury, but it seemed less a position of conviction than something encouraged by twilight-zone friends recounting their similar endowments. She was essentially smarter than that, but overwhelmed, baffled by the actual immediacy of the visions.

We looked at the posters in the windows of Avery Fisher Hall. In front of a reproduction of a blue Howard Hodgkins painting, Irina said, "Music paints the frame." An agility of mind gleamed like the picture itself, overlaid with the disjointed reflections of the city.

In contrast to her vision, to the unlit labyrinth down which she disappeared, there was in the night beside me the tangible, raiment-adorned presence of Irina, the weight of her breasts.

"Maybe one way of thinking about your visions," I suggested, "would be to assume that on their own they don't mean any more or less than any other aspect of reality."

"How would you do that?" she asked.

"You don't have to go outside the world to give importance to them," I said.

I quoted the clear lines of Zukofsky:

The order that rules music, the same
controls the placing of the stars and the feathers
in a bird's wing.
In the middle of harmony
Most heavenly music
For the universe is true enough.

In the attempt to offer a solution was also the impulse to dazzle, to lay it heroically at her feet. I was aware, too, that in part I was refuting the escapist stances of people she listened to, rivals for her attention.

"Visions are *images*," I said, "not the trippy evidence of some esoteric sparkler. The meanings they have — like everything else in the world — depend on the depth and discernment of our perceptions."

"All I know is they are real, they awful, and I have them," she said.

"Maybe you should let writing be what determines their importance. Poets have visions — look at Blake. Don't treat them as being any different from the rest of your imagination.

Irina sat at the kitchen table, smoking and staring out the window. She'd been uncommunicative all evening. I was making dinner.

"Wait'll you taste this. It's a Ron Johnson recipe," I said.

Her behavior resembled in its outward signs a sulking child whose ulterior motive, in the course of events, would be revealed. The difference was that in the black of Irina's moods nothing was visible. She didn't know what she wanted; or put another way, what she wanted, in an unsearchable dark, was for the connections that attached her to the syntax of knowing to be reinstated.

I set the silverware on the table, a blue napkin, a green napkin.

"What's this?" she said. "I'm not going to eat."

She got up and walked into the living room. "You go ahead," she mumbled, over her shoulder. An aloof pretension formed like frost around her.

I turned off the stove. She was sitting in a corner of the couch, looking through the pages of her notebook. I sat down beside her and ran my fingers along the edge of her foot. She pulled her foot away, propping her knees up to write on.

"What's wrong?" I said.

She concentrated on the hollowed-out space in front of her.

"What . . . ?" she said, after a long pause, lifting her eyebrows.

"Do you want me to ask you a simpler question?" I said, trying to make her laugh.

There was no response. I sat at the other end of the couch,

the sound of her pencil like a scratchy breath, as she made a doodle of aimless arabesques.

She sighed and closed her notebook.

"Why don't we try to translate something?" I proposed.

"Translate what?"

"I don't know — a Russian poem. It would be fun to do it together."

She considered the idea.

"Who would we translate?"

"It's up to you — whoever you think," I said.

She sat looking down at the floor, her chin on her knees.

"Should be someone famous?"

"It doesn't make any difference. You decide."

She rummaged through her purse, and took out some loose sheets of paper folded together.

"These are Blok. You know, Alexander Blok?"

She handed me the sheets, copies she'd made from a book, with both the Russian and English texts. I started to look at them.

"I don't think I should read the English translations — it would influence me too much," I said.

"I also have this Pasternak in Russian — without English," she said, holding up a small book. "I brought it. I don't know why. What kind of poem do we want? Pasternak writes different kinds."

She began looking through the book, at pages she had turned down.

"Well," she said, after a minute or two, "maybe this one. It's called 'Pines.' We could try. Let's eat first."

The black mood dissolved. It was like a scarf blowing off her shoulders.

"What are you cooking?" she asked.

"Tuna steaks — remember?"

"I'm hungry. What kind of wine is there?" Her face broke

into a smile, her eyes dancing. The tone of her voice dropped an octave, with mock Russian authority. "Is there any of that wine-dark wine?"

I bent down and kissed the top of her foot, wrapping my arms around her ankles. She laughed and squirmed away.

"Come on, I want some of that wine-dark wine!"

We finished setting the table, and Irina made a dressing for the salad, fretting with meticulous care over the balance of oil and vinegar. She put on a CD of Chet Baker singing.

"How did you make these onions? — they good!" she said. "Tuna should be rare. Other fish should be well done."

"I know," I said. "I got sidetracked."

"Don't pay attention to my moods. Don't take personally."

"It's hard not to."

"I would never want to hurt you — you most of all," she said. "You have to believe that."

We cleared the table. Irina sang little bits of "I've Never Been in Love Before." She sat down with a glass of wine and lit a cigarette.

"I'm going to quit," she said.

She put the cigarette out and lay her head sideways on her arms, bronze nails drumming softly on the table.

"I know — I am a lot of trouble," she said.

"We both are," I said.

The music ended, the last pellucid trumpet notes merging with a siren whining distantly through the city.

"Maybe we should try and see what happens," she said. "You know, with that Pasternak."

"Pines," the poem she had chosen, deals with a tender encounter between lovers. (Only later, retyping this, did I notice that the word "pines" is embedded in the word "happiness.") Irina was almost incapable of being romantic. She once pointed to a couple walking down the street in front of us with their arms around each other.

"I suppose you think that's what we should be like," she said, scornfully.

"They look happy," I said.

"They look *disgusting*!" she said.

The poem is like a little movie about longing. A couple, lying on their backs among lilies and chamomile in the sunlit clearing of a pine forest, inch toward each other in their minds.

We sat at the table, with Irina translating extemporaneously.

"*Grass . . . on piney footpath.* . . . Not 'footpath' — it's more like place fireworker goes in the forest. You know the word I mean?"

"I don't know . . . 'firebreak'?"

"Never mind, 'footpath' is good enough. Next line." She looks hard at the page. "*Unwalkable . . . and dense.* . . . What is it when you can't get through?"

"Impenetrable?"

"*Exactement*! Write it down!" she commands. "*Impenetrable and dense*. Next line. *We . . . exchange glances, and . . . once again* — next line — *poses and places*."

"They exchange poses and places?" I ask.

"That's what he wrote."

"It doesn't sound quite right."

"Are you going to argue with Pasternak?" she says, her face flush with authority.

"No, but something's wrong."

She looks carefully at the text.

"Maybe problem is in the rhyming word," she says. "Everything rhymes in Pasternak."

"Of course, that's it. We'll fix it. I think I know what he means."

In the next few stanzas, a silent buildup of delicate tension continues between the couple. The lines are unfolding before our eyes. We are a casual analogue to the poem, legs grazing under the table; I look at her face absorbed in thought, the lamplight on her cheek.

Just when one feels that the lovers can't for another moment restrain themselves, the poem pans away toward a veil of inter-connecting images.

Taller than these branches —
the tumbling crests of waves

"I know you'd like this, because of sea," Irina says. She twinkles with the knowledge of its surprise.

"Where did the sea come from?" I ask.

"Who knows? Russians are like that! Next line is, *Shrimp are raining down* . . . not raining, but . . . falling sort of. What is it when it's ice? — hail! *Stirred up from bottom of ocean.*"

"Shrimp?" I ask, incredulously.

"That's what it says."

"Is he painting a sunset with shrimp?"

She laughs. She laughs and laughs. Sometimes, not because what I've said is so amusing, but almost as a stylistic option, a behavior contained in the social canon of buoyancy, she dissolves in a spell of laughter.

There is, in fact, a sunset at the poem's conclusion.

Evening, a lingering dusk floats
on the corks of a trawler,
shimmering with fish shine
and the hazy smoke of amber.

It gets darker and slowly
the moon hides her track
beneath the foam's white
magic and the water's black.

The waves grow higher and louder
and on the dock the public stands
crowded around a kiosk poster —
indistinguishable at this distance.

The word "indistinguishable" is distance-embracing; I can hear the caress of its utterance in our night, ten floors above the streets of the city. It is the narrator's sly, understated expression of how exquisitely far from the eyes of the world the pine forest is.

"Let me read you what Pasternak says." Irina was sitting in the sunlight the following day, looking through a book she bought at The Russian Bookstore. "'The translation must be the work of an author who has felt the influence of the original long before he begins his work.'"

"They'll make an exception in my case," I said.

"How is that?" she asked.

"Because I know you," I said.

The sky was bright behind her with long striated clouds, leaving her face in shadow as she bent over the book, smiling. I knew Pasternak's poems only casually. My interest was not to see them into English but Irina's face, happy, across the table. Her own writing — the poetry she wrote in English — was a battle for coherence, notwithstanding the size of her talent. It left her bruised and defeated. No matter how careful I was to remind her of the awe I held her in as a poet, she occupied, solely in her eyes, a subservient role in our relationship as writers. Translating Pasternak reversed the positions: she had the upper hand, I was the supplicant. It gave her confidence and power, and had also the potential of breaking new emotional ground. Much of her life consisted of the manic traversing of disposable reality. Shallowness exerted an appeal precisely because its face value could be known and trusted. But here, through her own powers, serious work was being done (in which our tongues were linked!) that was difficult to impeach by the bias of her mind. She became lively, shy, unexpectedly virtuous.

"I get confused between what's junk and what isn't — that's problem of mine." We adopted a phrase, that she should be "where fine things are — where things are fine." Pasternak was a fine thing.

When I'd propose that we go to the movies or out somewhere, Irina usually voted to stay home.

"I don't want to go to movie," she'd say in a Russian pout. "Do you? What's playing? I only like that one, on Broadway, the little one — you know? — they have some good things sometime."

"Let's go there then."

"Not tonight. I was out all day. I bought beautiful yarns, the woman likes me, she old and brings out the different colors."

Either we'd cook (I would cook; Irina washed an occasional leaf) or we'd have dinner somewhere in the neighborhood. In the foyer of my apartment, a nearly life-size sculpture by James Lawrence stood like a sentinel facing the front door. Roughly carved out of a block of wood and painted in a loose, expressionist manner, it was a portrait of James Schuyler. Every night Irina walked in and hung her coat and hat on "Jimmy." She would arrange her shoes, come-fuck-me pumps, between his gay and indifferent feet. I tried to interest her in Schuyler's poetry, but she didn't respond to it. (She liked O'Hara and Ashbery.) Still, she dressed him up in her clothes, the great, unbalanced poet who walked naked once as Jesus Christ through the streets of Greenwich Village. (People are sane in so many different ways, and crazy in so few.) We went to a Fairfield Porter show to see the portraits of Jimmy, heavy-limbed in the summery green and gold of the Hamptons. He became for us — at home in the foyer — an icon devoted to Irina's success, with the knowledge that he had endured and written well to the end.

Heavy snow, thick flakes falling past the window where I write. I stare out at the descending snow and then glance down at the subtle image of its negative, like a veil lifting from a face.

This isn't a book of explanations; it counts the ways.

Johnny Hartman is singing "They Didn't Believe Me." Irina sits on the couch. "Is that Frank Sinatra?" Her toenails are violet. It is a coy, overly formal request, a child wheedling to win permission that she knows won't be withheld.

"Do you mind? I want just show you one poem. I wrote last night. O.K.?"

"Of course."

She walks on the couch, stepping over me and down to the floor, a flexed tendon, a shadowed area of inner thigh beneath her skirt sweeping past.

"Just one, I promise."

To pretend it requires guile to make it happen is rhetorical, against the time we spend day after day talking about and working on her poetry. It's part of a repertoire of wiles; but, most important in Irina's mind, it serves as a denial of the fact that we possess an intimacy that can be mutually presumed upon. "Intimacy," she says, "is one of my problems — intimacy and affection."

She returns with a dark blue file-folder, loose pages spilling out of it, and sits down beside me on the couch, glancing through her poems.

"*Un moment*," she says.

She goes into the kitchen and comes back with a glass of wine, which she sets on the floor at the end of the couch.

"Maybe this one," she says, handing me a page. "Wait!" She takes another look at it. "O.K., go ahead, but I don't think it's finished."

Her poems are often made by turning one event into another, a surreal enactment that takes place on the high wire of her associations.

"It's about us," she says.

When I finish reading it she reaches for the poem, saying, "Never mind, let me show you this other one."

"Wait a minute — I think it's terrific."

She kicks the glass of wine over.

"Oops! I always do that. I'll clean it up. Here, you can read these."

She does what all poets long to do: she writes directly from her unconscious. It isn't an amorphous overflowing of yearnings; she senses the outlines of a form — a pace and breath — and her images stun with unexpected lyricism, with the reach of originality. They're poems that look for themselves in uncharted air, they go like swallow flight, like great owls at night. This is what I see and what I say to her, in various ways again and again. "Now — what's wrong with them?" she asks. The process exhilarates her. She deepens her voice to a Russian command, "Tell me!" Her feet are in my lap. Hours are spent working on her poems, making suggestions, changes, following connections to other poets, examples, quotes that illuminate. She takes it all in, it's all about her, an endless need.

What's wrong with her poems is the same thing that's wrong with her life. They're a series of surreal, ungrounded images. "Hell has been proved to be a series of image," wrote

Jack Spicer. To the exact extent that she imposes on language the phantasms of her mind, she dismisses the presence of the world and its concinnity in the natural order of words. Gods that reside in the world's intimate relation remain unseen, untrusted — love, the god of the body, most of all. I recognize, perhaps even more than Irina, the importance of what her poetry could be, its "power," as Pasternak defines it, to align love and art.

    All this is unusual. All this absorbingly difficult.
    Taste teaches morality and power teaches taste.

The poems she showed me the day we sat beside the river were written directly in English. When he first came to America, Joseph Brodsky stayed with Robert Lowell and his wife, the writer Elizabeth Hardwick, and one of the things Lowell tried repeatedly to explain to Brodsky was that the kind of poetry he was writing came out in English sounding like doggerel. Irina was quicker than Joseph, with her savant-like ability to appropriate styles. We talked about line-breaks and stanzas, which she was eager to pin down as fixed, formal pattern. "This is what I need to found out about American poetry!" When I explained that it wasn't a rigid, repeatable construction but a form that evolved out of a poem's singular occasion, she blinked at it a few times, but began dauntlessly to imitate the examples I offered. After reading William Carlos Williams, several of her previous poems reemerged in step-down lines of threes. But the poems she wrote absorbed the notion that a poem has its own measure, beyond received forms and the indifferent melodies of free verse.

    What she couldn't do, finally, was make a poem cohere. (Pound's sad line: "I cannot make it cohere.") A friend of hers, a Russian poet, once said to me about the poetry Irina had written in Russian, "She has trouble with logic." Style can do almost everything but understand why it has happened. She'd show up carrying poems like broken dolls. At her clearest, she was aware that this was a different anguish, tied to an exalted process, a condition that involved her life at a profound and transforming level. The disorder in her thought was like a criminal who couldn't speak without confessing. It was present in overall composition, in the structure of sentences, in details of syntax. I'd make recommendations, and Irina would try to rewrite. Sometimes she'd be able to fix things, but usually it got muddy and slipped further away. Her talent, taste, and inclination created poems that demanded deftness. To teach himself what he needs to know is the poet's job, led in part by the difficulties his own failings set up. As Cavafy points out (in the quote book we began to assemble), it gives you the beautiful voyage.

Disorder was visible everywhere, especially in the continuity of day-to-day life. Rarely could anything be counted on to remain the same. Turmoil and exhausting doubt dominated the workings of her consciousness; plans were dissolved, decisions reversed, reference points revised. It was like a monkey house, their faces lined up in a row; when you glanced back they were dangling from the walls and ceiling.

Each night when she arrived at my apartment she reinstated distances, imposed a new formality. She stood at the door in her exquisite clothes like the line in *Nightwood*, with one hoof raised in the economy of fear. We lived in the same neighborhood, little more than a dozen blocks from each other, but rarely spent time together in her apartment. I met her there to help her move her desk. Long, loosely hung fabrics blocked out the sunlight in a small living room. A poster of Miles Davis, sleek and shirtless, was thumbtacked to the wall. There were two or three heavy pieces of furniture, but no place to sit. A French love seat, found in the street, with baroque bentwood arms, was piled with clothes, CDs, and papers, along with a framed photograph of Irina and a black man holding a saxophone. Past the kitchen, a long hallway led back to her bedroom, to the single bed and unexpected smell of incense — jealously scented — where we never spent the night, never made love. "*No one* stays here."

One evening she arrived at my apartment particularly distraught.

"Hello," she said, a stranger again, her smile fake and quickly wilting. The material of her dress was stiff with satiny sheen, falling around her in pink, pale orange, and cream-colored stripes. Every day her fingernails and toenails were a different color; tonight they were puce. She took off her shoes and walked into the kitchen.

"Do you have an ashtray?" she asked.

More than usual, her eyes shifted nervously over inner, indefinite distances.

"I'm not a writer. I don't want to be a writer."

"What's wrong?" I asked.

"Do you have any wine? Something red or — you know — white?"

Like a dissolve, the world of ashtrays and wine comes slowly into focus.

"Please, just take a look at this. It started out two poems. It was part of *Resurrection*, or perhaps something else, I don't know. But now I made it into one long poem. Because both poems were about same thing. Anyway, I destroyed it." She threw it on the table.

She sat beside me at the table, deeply upset, her face hard, moving on, sheering herself from the encumbering delusion of a life of meaning; it didn't exist. My job in the ritual was to find a way back — which brought with it the evanescent reward of her changed mood.

"It's awful, I hate it," she said. "I worked on this poem for three days. Do you know how long I worked on this? In Russia, when I wrote poem, I haven't slept. . . ."

"Shh — let me read it."

The pages were a mess of typed and scribbled lines. I could see how hard she'd worked. Connections had been worried with, narrative intent lost, forced into listless lines of confusion. What made her poems good was not the spectacle of her mental processes; that took away as much as it added. When there was clarity and a sense of shape her talent came through. Each poet is his own mad genius, "but the beauty / is not the madness." She sat at the table, smoked and mumbled curses, her mouth twitching grotesquely.

I took out lines, added and changed things; I shifted stanzas from one place to another. Her poems, more than most, benefited from moving things around; they came image upon image — the compositional energy less linear progression than something spatially deployed. Finally — after perhaps an hour — I came up with a tentative version. It was half the length and different in its order from what she had written, yet it was made out of her images, her startling voice. I read it aloud to her.

SYZYGY

I am calling it spring.
The fire is set
and I watch the pyre
of my death,
invisible papier-mâché of
flesh, burning
while the people
leave Brunnhilde's rock.

A woman in a checkered raincoat
chases the yellow
edge of the platform.
She is wearing my hat.

What do I know anyway
about this goddess.
Only children find
what they're looking for.
I can't even make the loop
hang down from the tree.

It frightens to have no fear.

I think of the moon, or time, or
no time.　　　I move.
She moves.　　I stop.
She stops.

High sky resembles a giant,
Wagnerian shadow. I jump into
a buttonhole of air.

　　　　I want
my flannel pajamas
back.

"That's it," she beamed. "That's what I meant!"

Stacked here and there in her apartment were large, atmo-
spheric collages that Irina made out of found images, totems,
mementos. Her method of writing was also collage-like. She'd
put down one thing and then beside it another, trusting the
connection between the two to materialize on its own. It cir-
cumvented logic. I worked on most of her poems. In some
cases it was little more than weeding out confusions; in others I'd rework passages that gestured haplessly toward an

effect, trying to rescue an intention. (If I asked Irina what she meant by a certain line, she'd recite the line verbatim, only in a slow, imploring tone. "A — ravenous — bird — cannot — live — in — the — bottle — of — ice — of — fire.") This took place on the spot between us — at home, on the subway, at the beach, on planes — as a mutual task, our faces inches apart, pens passed back and forth. From Shakespeare, Eliot, Pasternak, Pound, we set against the moods of negation that swept through her psyche precepts of towering authority that functioned at the same time as guideposts for how to write a poem. "What thou lovest well remains, the rest is dross." It made it twice as hard for Irina to deny their worth.

All her life she has moved from person to person, projecting onto the newest encounter the hope of her salvation. When it fails, as it invariably does, her next alliance represents both a renewed projection and, since the links are contiguous, a means of causing pain, of punishing the one who has failed. She hustles with a star-fucker's spite men whose rank, money, or power exceeds the limits of their predecessors. But the other side of this is the tragic awareness, through a glass darkly, that she can't sustain a deep relationship. The idea of an unblinking ardor, a continuous progression between simple tenderness and sexual love, is inconceivable. A derailment occurs. Her personality disintegrates and re-forms. She enters the world of the damned, where she assumes a stance of raffish hedonism, untouched by the sunlight of moral choice — where memory is a kind of confetti, falling in place.

The runway stride of her gait, her airs and clothes, the pretension of her bearing, her nutty utterances — she stands alone with these, one arm extended like Joan of Arc, the other clasped over a white breast. The fashion shot flip-flops between allure and lunacy, between sexual swank and girl absurd — soulless, binary. The weight, the baggage, the distance she has dragged it. In her daily negotiations with the world, she assumes a mask of elegance and superiority not in order to portray her life as something it isn't, but to master semblance itself — that's the extent of the enterprise, the measure of its success. Veils of being imprint her face like a Magritte, each with its transparent contradictions — the river we pull her from.

"I like to be near park, and this is Duke Ellington Boulevard. Look at that empty castle, with turrets and cupolas — it's great, yes?"

The boarded-up, long-uninhabited mansion on Central Park West was overgrown with wild vines and sumac trees. Part of the roof had come off, leaving an elaborate, spindly structure visible against the sky.

"It looks Russian," I said.

"Maybe we should fix it up and live there. What about that?"

As we passed another building with a brick bay front she said proudly, "My martial arts teacher lives here! He's a master." She did a kick into the air and then aimed her hands at me, crossed at the wrists. "This is Butterfly Defense — no one can penetrate it, not even Mohammed Ali. My teacher has Japanese girlfriend. They didn't live together, but now she moved in. He snaps his fingers, and she takes off her clothes. I'm just about to graduate, to get brown belt. You have to be approved to be in his class." An emotional confusion seeps into what she is saying. "They keep trying to get me to join them. He's passed through all the different planes — you know, planes of existence?" A few weeks later she told me that she'd spent an evening with them. They wanted her as the third in a sex trio. She didn't participate. "I watched them do it — that's all." It's hard to chart the firing of neurons in my own brain — jealousy, but jealousy defused by her hopeless gullibility; and hopelessness, mitigated by the thin thread of her candor. The stance of aloof sophistication that she affected gaped like a jack-o'-lantern. She was a little like Travis Bickle in the scene where he takes the respectable girl to the movies, unaware that not all movies are porno films. But she was lost in highs, in lows, and although I didn't realize it at the time, aside from an opaque innocence — a bubble in constant unbalance, with which she tried to make true the world of her experience — she longed for friendship like a marooned child. I even sensed (although I didn't want to think about it) that it was the Japanese girl who was important to her, who had been lost — not from a physical relationship, even if that had happened, but from a potential friendship that had somehow become impossible. Much later she said, "I don't care about woman sexually — I just wish I could have a friend." It didn't matter where they came from — where they came from was where she'd been. While she was working as an exotic dancer she had her clitoris pierced, a birthday present from one of her colleagues. "All you had to do was wear tight jeans and, you know, cross your legs — on the subway, anywhere — no one could tell." Her gynecologist, one of the most expensive in Manhattan, removed it.

Wet snow falls on the midnight border between millennia.

"I'm not feeling well," Irina said as she walked up the sidewalk to the restaurant, where I was waiting for her.

"What's the matter?"

"I should go home."

Her eyes, avoiding mine, shifted nervously without focusing.

"We don't have to stay if you don't want to," I said.

"Well, we're here," she said, impatiently. And then added, "You can't pet the cheetahs' royal heads."

"What do you mean?" I asked.

"*You—can't—pet—the—cheetahs'—royal—heads,*" she repeated. She hunched her shoulders and stalked into the restaurant.

When she said things like this — disconnected and delivered with a sense of profundity — it usually turned out to be a direct quote from a voice in her head. It was one of the forms her confusion took. The remark sounded totally bananas in part because it was baffling to her as well — uttered like a test of sense. It was a line of poetry, with links, occult but perhaps discoverable, to whatever had disturbed her.

She sipped her wine, looking at the menu. When the waiter came she said, "This red snapper . . . what is that . . . is it red snapper? I mean, what kind fish is it?" The meanings of the world lay in a slough beneath her.

"What upset you so much?" I said. "Try to tell me what it is."

"I — don't — know," she said, defiantly.

"Please, try. We can talk about it. We can deal with it together."

"This is *my* life, not yours!" she said, with poisonous hauteur.

She ate quietly, tiny bite-sized pieces of grilled snapper, her knife held between thumb and forefinger. Her perfect clothes, the silver blue of immaculate mascara. In its small clear glass, the white flame of a candle fretted back and forth.

"You get to share my life, but I don't get to share yours," I said.

"I don't have anything to share," she said.

"Share that," I said.

She lifted an eyebrow and with a weak breath blew a tiny explosion of air through her lips: *poof!*

Two nights before, I read her the finished version of "Pines." "It's great!" she marveled, and kissed me. "Congratulations to us!" We spent the rest of the evening translating a second poem of Pasternak's called "Autumn," with Irina consulting a large Russian-English dictionary, which she had brought with her. "Pasternak uses a lot of big words," she said, with delight. "Russian is great language!"

"Autumn" is about an older couple, living alone in a cabin. The family is dispersed. They have each other and the routine of their lives. The last two stanzas reveal the bedrock of the marriage.

You remove your dress
like a grove sheds leaves.
In a silk-tasseled bathrobe
you sink into my embrace.

You are the grace in the disastrous step,
when living is more tedious than illness.
The root of beauty is courage —
that is what draws us together.

Sitting across from her in the restaurant, I envied the poem's telescoping mood, its mopey, existential duration. The pride of complaint, lives lived together, the past survived, was like a thread withdrawn from the weave of our future: it would not be there.

The autumn couple that Pasternak's poem celebrates was mythic to me — a fixed star. I stumbled toward it in my life. Love isn't a standard that one can be held to. It's a direction. The straws that you grasp at are moral abstractions imposed from without. One is *in* love, in the sway of its giant, shape-shifting paws. There are mercies, but not justice.

Ratios within myself — of who and what I was — were changed in relation to Irina's extraordinary needs. Through no distinct virtue of my own, I could be of value to her life, simply by enumerating what it meant to be a poet and what it meant to belong to someone. Poetry and love, each so manifestly useless, took on a weight of purpose, a worth conferred by their place in the spectrum of her lacks. It gave an unforeseen dimension to feeling. Wings to desire. All the distances were in her.

She comes to bed in tiger-print shorts. A nightly transition occurs: one construct of Irina dissolves into another. The passage is subtle, ritualistic. She has to be seduced. "*Nnnno!*" — the coy voice of a fluttery damsel, glancing back, gypsy-eyed. The same stunning, unapproachable person whose fingertips cannot be touched lies naked in bed beside me. Before I slip her shorts off, down over long supple legs, I fold my hand over her cunt, clean-shaven and warm beneath the smooth, silky material — a contact (accepted by her body with unfazed equanimity) that represents pure obeisance, a gratitude luxuriating in sexual access, beyond the house of mirrors in her mind.

In her Park Avenue voice, Irina said, "Why don't we get out of the city for a few days?" A play I had written was, by a kind of fluke, in the process of being produced in an Off-Off Broadway theater downtown. Because I had to be there, I suggested that we go somewhere close to New York, but to a place neither of us had been before.

"Oh," she said, "this is play of yours? I didn't know you were playwright."

"I'm not. I wrote it a long time ago. I told you about it, remember?"

The play was a small musical I had written one summer for my daughter, which a friend of mine was putting together on a shoestring, in the hopes of attracting a producer.

"I guess," she said.

I could feel in her resistance a kind of overload. The information was — in the exigencies of her balance — somehow inconvenient. It required adjusting an image of me she had formed without it.

"Well, anyway, where are we going?" she asked.

It was our first trip, and Irina took an attentive and proprietary interest in planning it; we looked at maps, packed a few books. At Penn Station we ran into an old friend of mine, his wife, and their two young children. The station was packed with rush-hour travelers.

"Are you taking the Long Branch train?" my friend asked.

"Yes," I said.

"That's great, so are we."

Irina and I saw almost no one but each other. Recently I'd talked her into spending an evening with some friends of mine, a walk on the shore of the quotidian world. Time spent with other people was tantamount to a public acknowledgment of our being together; it trapped her in contradictions regarding intimacy. My friends, a painter and his novelist wife, lived in a comfortable apartment in the Village. The evening's domestic tone and casual conversation made her miserable. She glared at its sepia hue, said bizarre things, and when we left told me she would never go back again. "I hated them," she said.

In Penn Station she stood glancing nervously over the heads

of the swarming crowds. Her face, with its strong bone structure, betrayed inner shifts of agitation and fragility. Under the
best of circumstances it would have been inconvenient to be
intruded upon. Leaving the city behind and settling into the
intimacy of the train was a travel ritual. To miss it risked a delicate balance. Her eyes grew darker, more deeply shadowed,
scanning the panic at the edge of the horizon. With an omi-
nous sigh, she ran her hand through her hair.

"Why don't you kids show Irina what you got today?" the
mother coached, and then turning to Irina, said, "We can't go
to New York without stopping at F.A.O. Schwarz."

The track was called, and we all moved together toward
the platform. My friends were suburban, middle-class, mood-
demolishing. It wasn't Irina's terrain — children, domestic
energies. She was a visitor from another planet, a pythoness of
beautiful and lethal games. This was where the sleeve of fashion wore its rank — against the frumpy contours and hollow
comforts of New Jersey.

She walked like an important horse.

And then, in the train, she was surprisingly charming, open,
communicative; she played with the children, smiling shyly
at me. An hour later, my friends got off at their stop, and we
continued down the coast, the autumn sky darkening to dusk.
We arrived in a summery-looking sea community and after
searching around for a while found a place to stay, a pink hotel
close to the beach — almost a proud, rose-colored hotel.

Left alone, Irina slipped back toward a dead level of despair.
A portion of each time we met was spent in retrieving her.
But always, in the continuity of our days, she'd change, grow
clearer, happier — I swear it. I was naive and underestimated
the guile, the elusive tenacity of irrational rule. Still, it happened, her smiles were real. I don't credit my influence unduly;

any influence would have produced an effect — she was lost, cyclonic. But to tie the promise of her life to poetry — to a credible belief in the importance of her talent — presented a difference she was unaccustomed to. Half the time what she found on her own in "quick fixes" or hippie-simplistic "answers" were, in their flimsy utility, nothing more than a confirmation, a devious choreography, of what she dreaded.

Her mind moved in circles, not forward. Any time spent apart — a day, even a few hours — carried with it a revised anonymity, a nightly unraveling, as if everything heretofore known about her were by tacit pact suspended and she was free to invent and reveal a new version of herself, the contradiction of which would amount to inexcusable rudeness. Still, what we were and did and hoped represented, however provisional, a net gain. On the cover of a slender notebook, which she brought with her on our trip, she'd written in design-like cursive the word "Resurrection." Escape and surcease, a breath she could take in a continuing predicament where, as in Mahler, hope battled to remain an option, were also travel plans. Good visions. Promised lands.

It was too cold to swim, but we went for walks along the beach, the ocean festive with weightless lights. On a gray, salt-weathered bench, sheltered from the wind by dunes and grasses, we sat in the sun and worked on her poems. We were getting somewhere. Happiness was being proved possible, on terms she had not considered. In the hotel we had an L-shaped room with a brass bed and, in the small living area, a white wicker couch. A cutout wooden flamingo stood in one corner. Irina wore black slacks with red silk flames rising up from the cuffs. Travel produces a kind of intimacy; you float beyond yourself, bound only by each other. I don't know exactly how long we'd been together at this point — a couple of months maybe — but long enough for me to realize that to make love Irina depended upon a ritual of seduction, a mechanism that entailed the appearance of the subversion of her will. One time, in a particularly chaotic mood, when she first started spending the night at my apartment, she said, "It should happen when we're asleep — and wake us up." By now, the ritual of seducing her had begun to feel unnatural, anachronistic; it wasn't at all a sustaining of magic preliminaries, which would have been welcome, but more the ordination of a stunted dance devoted each time to conquering her anew. It was connected, of course, to the snarl of everything else in her life, but it seemed at this moment, with muted sea-light coming through the pale curtains, that if her lover could be acknowledged fully in the grammar of her will, a step might be made toward a mature intimacy. She listened, thoughtful, assenting in tentative nods to what I said. When I kissed her there was a different yielding, without coyness, the closeness itself embraced. Her eyes met mine for a flickering instant as we undressed.

In bed, she was like an exquisite dancer. She anticipated every lead, performed with supple and deft ardor, with intricate attenuation, a seamless sexual arabesque. Her body, her long legs and firm, round breasts, her mouth became a field of saturation in which her identity was submerged. But the psychological space she inhabited was private. Her eyes were closed. There were never shared gazes, through veils of ecstasy.

The hand that folded around my penis, the delicate pressure and caress that held it as she took it into her mouth, belonged solely to the expertise, the finely orchestrated requirements of the dance. Her mouth was soft. I could feel the faintest forming and release of its bond as her lips slid over the glans and down the side of the shaft. My hands were in her hair. Every time we made love I was aware of the balance between her physical presence and her lost, withheld self. It followed a strangely calibrated etiquette between pleasure and retreat. There was compliant, glorious participation, but not abandon. Her orgasms were silent, or only rarely signaled by a muffled, sob-like moan, when she was drunk.

"Did you come?"

"Yes."

"When?"

"In the middle."

I kissed her breasts, feeling her rib cage rotate beneath me, her slightly arched back. It didn't matter where we started. We inhabited a sexual sphere; nothing could be lost. With nuzzling adoration I licked her belly, soft as water. I pressed my lips against the smooth wet flanges of her labia, tonguing alternately her clitoris and the saline dark of her vagina. Her hips floated up from the bed. As I began to penetrate her she made a soft, audible cry. The delicious entry, the slow perfected movements, equal and rhythmic, passed like waves over us. "Open your eyes," I said. For a moment there was no response, only the beautiful, closed face, jolted softly by the insistent action of our bodies. "Irina?" Her eyes fluttered open, evasive and wild for a moment, and then looked steadily into mine. Don't say it. Don't breathe it. Smother it in her hair. Her arms pulled me toward her.

Afterwards, we lay in the disappearing light. I watched the rise and fall of her stomach.

"Why don't you stop shaving your pubic hair?" I said.

"You want me to?"

"Yes."

"You have to shave to be dancer. They won't take you if you don't."

"You're not a stripper anymore."

"Thanks God!" she said.

"It would be a way of saying that's over, and this is real."

A clock ticks on the repose of lovers' bodies; they belong to each other only so long.

"You are *right!*" she said, with rhetorical exuberance and dashed across the floor into the bathroom.

On the train back to New York she began to tell me about her childhood.

"My brother started — you know — doing to me. It happened on our red couch. We would pile up pillows into a house. My mother almost caught us one time. She came in and we were naked."

"How old were you?"

"Four."

"How old was your brother?"

"Eight or nine. He couldn't do much at first. He'd get on top of me and move around. But it went on for several years. We slept in same bed."

"What about your parents?" I asked.

"They didn't know. But then they sent me to live with grandmother," she said. "They didn't want — you know — to confront."

According to Irina her father came once a year to visit her.

"I remember. He never hugged me, and never kissed me."

"What about your mother?"

"I don't know. I studied violin," she said.

Beach towns slipped past us in the dark with waves like paisley shawls lying on the empty, moonlit sand. The trip had made us closer. The person I'd glimpsed behind the disarray of craziness and defenses had grown more visible, more present, dearer. Sitting beside her in the small isolated space of the train, I was prepared to take on her nemeses.

"This is probably what's behind everything," I said. "A small girl's revenge on her betrayers. The child that you were — the four-year-old Elvira — is still essentially who you are, frozen, enacting scene after scene of terrible vengeance. No wonder you changed your name."

"What do you mean?" she asked.

"As a child, you know innately that you belong to your mother and father, that you matter to them because you're theirs. But you're just a kid, without any power. So the only part of them that you can hurt is yourself. I think that's what's happened."

I'm saying these things with naive and soaring animation, as if the act of divining the connections could undo the evil spell. While we were in New Jersey she dreamed she was six years old in a violent storm. "It was thundering and lightning and I was naked, begging to be obliterated."

Out the window, the skyline of New York came into view, like an ad for reality.

"Do you know how you can punish them most?"

"Who?"

"Your parents and your brother."

"How?"

"By being happy."

The idea startles her. She begins to write in her notebook.

"No one ever told me this before! It's like two years of therapy" — she snaps her fingers — "in one train ride!" She'd been in therapy at some point before we met, but had deceived the therapist by concealing her problems. "It was a waste of money — I quit." As we pull into Penn Station, she's in an expansive mood, as if — epiphany in place — she could march into the storm and told the monstrous child in her arms.

We walked quietly side by side past the black girders on the empty platform, her body leaning into mine, my arm around her hips.

On the subway home, she said: "That part about hurting herself — I've got it, I understand — just tell me again how that works."

Like others, the epiphany got lost. In an insidious shifting of sand, it became associated simply with my position, something I invoked as a key to conflicts and therefore not any truer than I was. An inflexible power monitored her movement toward the light. To name it "Elvira," to expose its workings in her life was information that, once expressed, changed nothing. It disappeared into a maw of psychic wounds. Our conflicts were quickly co-opted by the mechanism I'd hoped we could together oppose. With my abstractions, my books and poems, I was no better than the gangsters and their bags of money. I sat beside her one night, when she had fallen into bed exhausted, and listened to my voice grow hollow, fustian.

Not how they fit, but that the pieces do, is the puzzle.

On the white sheet, her head tosses from side to side, eyes closed, whimpering, her brow flexed in a rush of sensation: image — also — of the doomed resistance of a child. She grew her pubic hair into a small, artfully trimmed shape. "Do you like it like that?" she asked. "It's beautiful," I said. "But it itches," she said.

A passage in Proust about Mademoiselle Vinteuil and her father, something by Ben Jonson, a poem of Robert Creeley's (of all the contemporaries, Creeley was her favorite), a line from *Malte Laurids Brigge* — the daily array of our conversation is a kind of literary provender. Her life is a term in the skein of blown silk, a meaning of mermaids' song. Lovers read "Asphodel."

> In the huge gap
>   between the flash
> and the thunderstroke
>   spring has come in
>   or a deep snow fallen.

We occupied, in a way, a similar interval. The cosmic struggle between light and darkness that Williams depicts in the coda of "Asphodel" wasn't simply an intrinsic condition of her life; her evasions of reality raised the stakes until nothing could be understood except in elemental terms. *She* was a storm. Her problems refused to stoop to individual solutions; they were bound together in mute defiance, demanding resolution at some primal, inhuman level where she was poised to fail. This was the secret, ruby-dark stratagem, the heavy tumblers in the lock, to wring from the gods an impossible compassion. At large, at lunch, in the ghostly touch of her hands.

She had good days and bad, and good days had bad moments. She was hounded by split-second mood swings — levitating on a froth of rapid associations that dissolved, at normal speed, into nonsense and despair. For short stretches she could be fine — bright, forthcoming, energetic — "I'm completely present." But the days were made of waves that crashed over her.

My moods could be toppled also. With her mercurial changes, rejection was around every corner. At times the tiniest word could destroy me. My emotional resources would simply disappear. I could hardly lift my arms. The defeat I felt was like a child's desolation: I had been shot out of the sky. "You have this issue," she said, with perspicacity. We limped in lockstep. Yet, when she changed, it was often without recourse to why.

"I'm interested in purity — purity of heart. It's kind of, you know, spirituality." She spoke in the distant and formal tone of a first encounter.

"We've met before — remember?"

She took a sip of her wine, and turned her face away from me.

I said, "When you start to talk about purity, I can tell you're in trouble."

She agreed, "I'm in the traffic by then."

Williams is wrong in his interpretation of certain parts of the Unicorn Tapestries at the Cloisters. He sees two unicorns in the sixth tapestry when in fact it's the same unicorn seen at different times — at the moment of the kill, and then later, slung over the back of a horse. He also thinks of the unicorn in the final tapestry as a third, who has survived the hunt, rather than the resurrected form of the one. As his correspondent, A.G., liked to say, "You don't have to be right."

In the train on the way to visit the tapestries, we read out loud to each other the fifth book of *Paterson*, with its clear-hearted delineation of the whore and the virgin — "both for sale / to the highest bidder!" The sexual element that shadows every stage of Irina's experience has been so consistently a term of transaction that she is, in a way, untouched. But her life is tangled in depths that exceed irony. Her brother's sex with her as a child not only betrayed and skewered the trust of a primary relationship, it cheated her out of the ecstatic moment of surrendering her innocence. Her virginity could not be offered to the first real lover in her life, and so, in the coils of guilt, shame, and punishment, its absence is continually resold in a marketplace where each lover will always be outbid because none can ever pay enough. (And if her brother is seen as her first lover — "I enjoyed it" — then his inevitable abandonment of their intimacy is an added betrayal.) What Williams's poem contends — or what I, as we walk through the echoing Cloisters, contend on its behalf — is that the whore and the virgin are identical in their distance from the realities of love between a man and a woman, and that the imagination, which conceives of love, of words to sing its palpability, is a world separate from a deadweight accounting system that divides fucking anybody and fucking nobody into faults and virtues.

The idea of coming here was to see in person the source of Williams's text. When we first read the poem, she said, "This is poem about me. These are my issues." When I told her that the tapestries were housed at the Cloisters, a subway ride away, she insisted that we go. Yet now, sitting on a stone bench, with cool silver light invading her face, she is distracted and without focus.

"Remember when Williams talks about the first phase of sexual desire? He calls it 'a moral gesture.'"

"So?" she says.

"It's like Pasternak's idea about 'the cleanest of all things.'"

She doesn't answer.

"If someone is deprived of that first phase, that clear moral gesture, it's possible that they lose not only the tender incandescence of love's beginning, but its presiding star, so to speak, at the beginning of every possible love."

"I think you're right," she says, remotely. "That sounds true."

"So" — I smile a simpleton's smile — "now that we know that, you're free to start over. Because it never happened is exactly why it still can."

Her face is tense and somber. I touch her hair. The splendor of the tapestries surrounds us.

"The girl who waits in the woods — who is you, my darling

zaichik — is the incarnation of that moral gesture." She stares out the doorway at the garden, with dull eyes. "All the fabulous pageantry, the whole goddamn story of love, depends on it — wildflowers, hunters, the pack of hounds, and the incredible white animal, whose horn rises unashamed from his head like the spiraling thought that thought him up."

I lean forward to kiss her. She pulls away — I kiss the air.

Only fragments remain of one of the tapestries, which appears to depict the moment of encounter between the girl and the unicorn. All you can see of the virgin is her fingers, sensual and lively, in the unicorn's mane. The damage to this tapestry is like an allegory of Irina's life — the ravaged fabric at the advent of love.

no woman is virtuous
who does not give herself to her lover
— forthwith

This Irina couldn't do; she couldn't give her heart. She lacked the moral authority, and so could never possess the power and illumination that derive from surrender. That night at home I listened to her talk, the easy timbre, the lisp of her accent that pronounced "earth" as "earf," the ever-present disarray of associations, which broke now and then into self-conscious laughter. It was a voice that broadcast a persona of innocence, ardent and gently hopeful.

"This is who I think you really are," I said, "the way you are right now."

She blew air through her teeth and made a face. I kissed her forehead, my hand cupping her cheek. The candle in the tin chandelier floated shadows on the ceiling above the couch.

"Let's try something," I said. I continued to kiss her, lighter than a breath.

"Try what?" she said.

"Make love to me right now. Exactly as the person you are this moment."

I ran my fingers over her breast, looking into her eyes.

"Don't change. Just make love to me," I whispered.

Her body heaved wearily, as she pushed herself up, away from me. She stood beside the couch, her eyes bleak, averted.

"I can't do that. You know I can't do that."

Angrily, she crossed the room and began putting on her shoes to go home.

"Why are you trying to make me *do what I can't do*?" she screamed.

"Irina, we make love every night."

"Not *every* night," she said.

I watched as she slumped forward over her shoes. They lay on the floor in front of her, green spiked heels, their loose ties like flags on musical notes. She sat staring into space, not any less lost for being able to make her predicament a term of emotional negotiation. Used like any other cliché, with the same unconscious facility, it was a momentary window, a pause to leverage the option of not having to make real the threat of leaving. It would have only a fleeting life — in the next moment she would be gone.

I got up and sat beside her.

"Don't go home. Stay here, where you belong," I said.

"I don't belong anywhere," she said, with sweeping drama.

"Yes, you do. Calm down."

She leaned away from me.

"I don't like these shoes," she said. "They Italian, you know, the Italians? They green like leezards."

"The Italians are green?"

She clamped her lips together to suppress a giggle.

"They make green *shoes*," she said, ". . . and green noodles . . . and green olives!"

I put my arm around her. She sat quietly without resisting.

"I would love to go to Italy with you someday," she said.

"Let's go," I said.

"I have just two, maybe three things I need to work on, to get straightened out in my mind. When I do, then we can be together, you know, in real way."

"Is that what you want?"

"You know it is."

Innocence, kind and unadorned, that nested intact within the gloss of her sexual exterior was the elusive element, the narcotic that burned in the air of every touch. Two hours later, in bed, the bottom of her foot rakes lazily over mine. When I kiss her, her arms move with sleep-heavy slowness, to hold me. The entire tension of the evening, like an elaborate, torturous pursuit, is concentrated in our bodies. I have an immediate, immense hard-on, which her fingers hold like a velvet sleeve, sliding off. I rub the nipples of her breasts with the top of my penis. Making little breath-caught moans, she slides down until it is in her mouth. I curl around her, the ecstatic sensation, the soft and delicate expertise of her tongue combine in an enormous relief, a cascading absolution of unity achieved, of contact. She pushes me down onto my back, arching over me, her head rising and falling, taking it deeper into her throat, like a sword swallower. When I try to pull her up beside me, to enter her body, she resists with firmness. One hand passes feather-like along the crease of my anus, the other slips around my waist, holding me with redoubled intensity. I come in her mouth. The force of the orgasm gradually subsides, diminishing in resurgent spasms, to a still point. Only then does she break the connection. She climbs up into my arms, and lies on top of me. The moment's refulgence clings like a rare raiment of silk.

"Do you want to take shower?" she says.

"Not yet. This is too lovely — you are."

She rolls over and props herself up on one arm, her black eyes wide awake.

"You taste like mint," she says.

A corrosive light passes through the partitions; incidents mark out a geometry, like islands on a map. You can look at it from saffron shallows, where pungent, rust-purple weeds dry in the sun. The angles break off from each other into a pattern of planes, as if from a great height. The smell of candles, deli-flowers, and Badedas.

"Let's try to do another Pasternak," she said. Our translations followed a routine. Irina would say what she thought a line said — wrestling in midstride with the robust morphing of Pasternak's language — and I'd write it down. Sometimes she had only a vague idea of what was happening in the poem and would simply state the literal order of the words — "Go ahead, put it down, we'll find out later." She'd stop and fill her wineglass. Sometimes, hearing the words unfold, I'd perceive a structural intention, and a sense of the line would come to me first — which she would either confirm or grandly reject. We continued line by line until a crude draft was set down, which I would then work on by myself over the next several days. Irina's participation was like a performance, heady, dramatic, spot-lit, lasting two or three hours.

We had completed three poems — "Pines," "Autumn," and "Frost" — when I noticed their order mirrored the order of the seasons we'd been together: summer, autumn, and winter. This wasn't something Irina would ever consciously have done. It was too sentimental, too adroitly commemorative. But in her case unconscious decisions were the rule — life trailed out magically, or perilously, in their wake — so we took it as a propitious sign, even if, or rather because, the oracle was herself. The poems didn't serve as masks for her feelings; they were, in fact, more like surrogate feelings. Sails hung in unmoving air. To express affection (a rare occurrence), Irina used, if not masks exactly, oblique gestures, symbols. She made at various times tapes of classical music for me — in part because I knew almost nothing about it — a great amalgam of passages from Tchaikovsky, Rachmaninoff, Saint-Saëns, Mahler, Ravel. On each tape she'd write in an elegant diagonal "For Bill" and draw beneath it a heart, or a pair of red lips. "I'm making you a new *tape*," she would say, sitting in candle shadows on the wide print-covered couch, her skirt tucked up under bare legs. There was an understanding that the tapes meant something, but in the unstable atmosphere of mood reversals, it was equally understood that they meant nothing.

The poems Irina picked out were applicable to us only in the same way that any other selection of poems might have been.

Frost

Muffled time of leaf fall,
the last vees of geese;
don't get upset — all
fear has wide eyes.

Let the wind that lulls the ash
scare her before she sleeps.
Creation is deceptive,
like the ending of a fairy tale.

Tomorrow you will wake,
walk out onto the winter sheen
behind the water pump
and stand rooted in the scene.

Again those white flies,
rooftops and Christmas rooms,
chimneys and the lop-eared woods
dressed in Joker's costumes.

At once, everything whitens,
in a *papakha* up to the brows.
A stealthy wolverine
peeks through the boughs.

Uncertain, you cross the yard,
the path plunging down a gully
to a gingerbread house of frost,
its doors and windows barred.

Inside, behind the snow's
thick curtain, on the wall of
a kind of cabin, a road goes
past a clearing, to a new grove.

The solemn stillness
set in fretwork
resembles a quatrain on the tomb
of Sleeping Beauty.

To the kingdom white and dead
which sends shudders through me,
quietly I whisper, thank you,
you give more than is demanded.

I could glimpse in the beautiful icy kingdom of "Frost" a
metaphor for Irina's emotional state, but to read into any of
the poems aspects that resonated excessively with the details
of our lives would have been to diminish them. Our involvement was aesthetic and collateral. The poems were folded into
the general flow of things. We added them to our mythos.

"What's a *papakha*?" I asked.

"You don't have them here. They kind of Russian hat — soft and furry."

I sent her a postcard, "I love your *papakha*." The card ended up as an element in one of her collages.

The idea of translating Pasternak involved for Irina an indisputable value. Her face at the kitchen table, focused beyond itself — as it so seldom was — is the *Vogue* cover I'll frame. She read the poems aloud in Russian, conscientious in her delivery, the sibilant gristle of words and the soft music of her voice. These were our nights, our dominion. They led to the world outside her head; they led to bed. We walked in the park at midnight, the luminous snow silent, cloud-lit. Poetry connected us, not as an exalted condition, but as a fact of our affinity. To be a part of one another's society involved a different set of assumptions, a different rain pinging on the air conditioner, as we stacked the dishes in the sink. I loved her for reasons known and unknown, but unquestionably because she was a poet. The place Pasternak held in the Russian imagination gave authority to poetry per se. She could resist but not refute it. It was a fulcrum in her assent to think differently of her life. "You are so willing to define yourself as a stripper, or a thug's mistress, or a violated child, or a crazy person," I argued. "But if you believe you are a poet, then everything else, no matter what, is simply part of how you have become one."

An incidental parallel could be drawn — albeit in fantastic ink — between Pasternak's life and my own. An early involvement through his mother in music; the original intention to become a composer; the shift in his late teens to writing — my life followed an almost identical pattern. It is of course an absurd comparison — the Texas burlesque of a serious destiny.

In the family living room Rosa performed Rachmaninoff's newest compositions, while young Boris listened. Scriabin was his music teacher, Rilke and Tolstoy family friends. Yet poets are each other's standard, beyond squalor, madness, or privilege. A new century had begun. We sat up late, the city half-dark, a deep-eyed, moon-troubled girl and I, turning Pasternak's poems into English.

The things we did together, no matter how innocently pursued, were also the torches we used to search the dark of each other. We met, in a way, like mirror images. What was particular in betrayal and loss formed in each of us a hand that matched the other's — whose fingers touched and drew back, in perplexed recognition. The torque of unrelieved strain, to possess the unpossessable, extended to the smallest incidents in our lives. The barrier itself was thrown into relief — on each side of which stood lovers riven from themselves. Fears and vulnerabilities that I had learned more or less to manage or finesse into shadows loomed like full-scale X-rays of myself, independent of Irina precisely because, in the broadest sense of the word, she was not responsible. On some level every encounter in which a woman is contested for reruns in my emotional makeup a drama of inevitable loss. Men, unknown and omnipotent, capable at the slightest whim of taking her away from me, pass like phantom threats across the drawn shade of my childhood. Irina's immunity to emotional symmetries, her willingness to do harm without conscience, left me powerless in a similar way, making one the resonating structure of the other. Night and memory — its poisonous bloom. That a part of her attraction had always been the broken, the half-whole, corresponded with an ingrained self-doubt that sees only the deficient as prey. It was true, but it was something both revealed and subsumed in deeper contrasts. From her childhood on, she immersed the whole concept of love in flaunted and defiant self-abasement. Whereas in my formative mind its essential definition, its sole access, was genital. A holy prowess conquered in the dark.

My eyes pass over the objects in the room — the chairs, table, books, the black phone with its angular sheen. It's a kind of half-seeing, a marking by duration, random as an eclipse. Irina had called at seven-thirty. "*Hel-lo*," the descent a perfect third, tender as the night. "I'm running bit late. I'll be there by eight, let's say eight-thirty — O.K.? No later than nine, I promise."

"Where are you?" I asked.

"Right now?" she said.

"Yes."

"Well . . . I'm at gym. I have to stretch — you know? It's good for you."

It's now after ten. I look at the lamp, its cocoon of light, the corner table, the small square clock — a turned-to aggregate of the inanimate.

The abyss opens, increment by increment. A spiraling agitation takes over my senses. In flashes of chimerical detail I see her averted face, the hair on his shoulders, her doll-closed eyes. The vision is a flimsy, self-taunting affliction that I can renounce but not control. I'm aware also that what happens to me in these moments is something more encompassing than jealousy. Like a miser, I unfold the velvet cloth and gaze at the poisonous gold. It isn't a total corruption of trust; it is instead simply the daily standard of its challenge, imposed by my own fears and weaknesses. The specters are freighted with the inauthentic; only in that is their torment assured.

Outside is the city's presence, its piping voices, the glittering of its unknowable hedonism — of which somewhere she is a part. In the hollow room of time I can feel the pull of the negative, like a dead level of who and what I am.

The elevator door opens and closes in the hall. As she walks into the apartment her eyes are bright with excitement.

"It takes longer than I thought," she said. "Are you mad?"

Before I can answer she removes from her bag a long, elegant scarf and wraps it around my neck. She fluffs the material, fussing with how it looks.

"It's good color, I think. Do you like it?" she asks,

The scarf is a deep empyrean blue, with flecks of white scattered in it like stars.

"It's beautiful," I said.

"Are you sure you like it?"

"Yes."

"Well, I made for you. I had to finish today."

"You *made* it?"

"Of course. It's silk and mohair. You know — mohair?" She takes another loop over my head with it. "It's long! You have to wear like this."

"You are an incredible woman," I said, putting my arms around her. "More than I deserve."

"It's poet's scarf," she said.

"How did you learn to do this?"

"From grandmother," she said.

Irina was running out of the money she'd saved when she worked as a stripper. She didn't openly tell me about it or ask me outright to help her; instead she performed a charade, made up of transparent statements, baldly designed to elicit an offer of assistance. It was what she knew how to do. She also implied indirectly that I bore a responsibility for the situation she was in.

"I wouldn't have this trouble before," she said sullenly.

I made most of my living, sporadic as it was, as an art consultant. I juggled the demands of making ends meet with staking out time to write. At the moment I was living almost entirely on credit cards, dividing my energies between the play that was being produced downtown, itself a slim but possible source of income, and Irina. This was a crisis I had dreaded. On the one hand, I was afraid that I literally might not have the money to help her. But my chief fear, as I wrote her a check, was how she would interpret it — or more precisely, how to keep her from processing it as a repetition of the roles her past relationships had conformed to.

"Please, don't get confused about this. Don't try to rearrange it in your head and turn it into a transaction. We're together. Do you understand?"

"Yes."

She is silent for a moment, her eyes empty, like a sedated predator.

"*I'm* going to do something."

There is a livid threat in her voice.

"What are you going to do?"

"I know what I have to do."

The polished theatrics only make it sadder, more tragic.

"What — go back and work as a stripper? Listen, it's exactly now, in moments like this, that you have a chance to make something different happen in your life. I'm here, I'm with you." I touch her fingers, locked together in front of her on the table. "You already know where all the wrong choices lead. You end up hating yourself."

"I hate myself," she says.

"I can't give you cars and Cartier watches. I'm not a Mafia guy. But I think I can give you something else, something better. And it will really be yours. No one can take it away from you."

"You know I value what we have."

"Just decide two things. That we're really together, and

that it is up to us — not you by yourself — to face and deal with whatever the problems are. We'll figure it out."

"But, Bill, you can't take care of me — you barely have enough money to do for yourself."

"It's not a question of how much money I have. It's a question of whether we love each other or not."

"I do love you, you know that."

"We can make it work. People do it every day. And then you can respect rather than hate yourself."

"Do you know how much my rent is? This is America! If you don't pay rent, they throw you out! That's all to it!"

"We'll manage. We can live together in one apartment if we have to," I say.

"I'm not going to be starving artist — that's for sure!" She gets up from the table, on her way back to thousand-dollar nights. "There's a doctor who'll buy me condo. He's married. Actually, he just wants to stop by once or twice a week. Something like that — you know?"

She paces around the apartment, her face tense and clouded.

"Society teaches you to be a whore," she says. "You don't understand spirituality. You don't understand purity. *PUR-I-TEE!*"

"Sit down and listen to me for a minute. You can get a real job, in the real world. We can do this together, Irina."

"What about my 'moods' — who's going to hire me?"

"We'll find someone for you to see — a good doctor. There are medications that'll help."

"I want to go away and be monk — live in the mountains."

She returns to the table and lays her head on her arms.

"Please, listen to me. Just the decision to do this will stare down a lot of demons."

"Will it stop the noise in my head?"

"Yes — the medication will."

Her arm rises up into the air like a wand, and then falls limply onto my shoulder. I lean over and kiss her hair, which is short and the orange color of sea-coral.

"Purity isn't a literal fact, like sitting in a cave away from everybody," I say.

"What is it then?"

"It exists in the same way any other meaning exists."

"Like what?" she asks, grudgingly.

"The way water in a poem can also be a woman. It's not about the facts of reality, they mean nothing on their own. You can sit in a cave for the next ten years and still be corrupt. But when water becomes a metaphor for woman, it's pure in a way no snake can ever perceive."

"Not everyone is a poet."

"But you are."

"No, I'm not. I've given up writing."

Part of every day is spent on this scaffolding. These are prolonged, elaborate conversations sprinkled with panic, with darting maledictions from the maze. Yet in them I can sense something else at work, unnameable, beyond her recalcitrance and fear, that gives to the whole performance a gauzy misdirection, as if a separate purpose were being served, an intravenous drip funneled to some secret cavity of her ego. Madness flexes its dominion. Being with Irina is harder than being with anyone else I have ever known. She's almost incapable of resolving the smallest conflict. Her attention can't and won't focus on particulars; she shifts to unconnected associations and then, tangled in the clashing logic that tries to retrieve her, shuts down belligerently. Our arguments rarely center on issues; she cuts off the possibility of speaking with a long stream of babble. I wait for it to stop. She stares at me in the silence. As soon as I open my mouth she begins again.

After long, enervating bouleversements — "My bank is

empty, I can't get a job, I'm not doing this, I hate those people" — she at last agreed to see a doctor. My hope was that medication would help her. I had the same misgivings about "those people" as she did. Yet I felt that her consent to try to face her problems, rather than continue to allow them to drag her into the same destructive orbit, was by itself a beneficial step. I also didn't know what else to do.

We spent the next couple of weeks going from one bureaucratic office to another, to get her admitted into the city's mental health program. We filled out forms in grim waiting rooms, Irina distraught and overdressed, constantly threatening to back out. It was like changing the course of a tanker in midocean.

"Grigory, my artist friend — you saw his paintings. He's from Russia — you know. He lives completely off rich patrons," she said.

"Grigory is a whore," I said.

"I know that," she conceded. "He's not even good artist."

A few weeks earlier, she had told me about an incident involving someone Grigory had introduced her to at a gallery opening. He was a man in his sixties, who owned houses in Aspen, New York, and the Virgin Islands. His name, as she showed me, was among the list of benefactors etched into the wall at the Metropolitan Museum. The day after they met, "The Benefactor," as she called him, came to her apartment. He walked in and took all his clothes off, suggesting she do the same. "Let's get to know each other," he said. She asked him to leave. When she told me this it had the tone of a confession; she felt uncomfortable concealing it from me. He arrived like an incarnation of the welter of her past, a devil appearing on her doorstep: *"Did you think you could escape?"*

"What happened?" I asked.

"I would never sleep with him," she said with indignation.

Then from the same brain:

"Or if I did, it would be with a *condom!*"

"So what did he do?"

"Nothing. He left. Well . . . he gave me key to his house in Aspen. He said, 'Go out there whenever you want.'"

"Did you give it back to him?"

"No, he just left. I'll give key to Grigory."

I felt helplessly jealous. It was as if the key were a kind of contamination, hosted by unexpressed affinities. Yet she seemed as disturbed as I, protective of our trust, which was itself a new attitude.

It was cold and bleak the day of her first psychiatric interview. Tops of skyscrapers disappeared into thick low clouds. The psychiatrist's office was located in a massive housing project on the West Side. It looked like Soviet Russia. Her life was beset by gratuitous possibilities of money and glamour. Benefactors sought her out. That we lacked the resources for her to choose an independent doctor made the dingy rooms and faceless clerks, the degrading and inane procedures imminently vulnerable to her contempt. I felt powerless. If under such circumstances she was able to follow it through, the strength of the decision would be hers.

"Her name is Dr. Valdes," she said.

"Don't worry," I said. "This is just a formality to get you into the system. I'll be there, we can talk to her together."

We sat in a waiting room with half a dozen dreary, empty-eyed people, middle-aged Latino men in work clothes, a frail African woman with patterned scars on her face. When Irina was called she said, with calm resolve, "I'm going by myself — just wait for me." Fifteen minutes later she returned.

"Well, I'm in the system," she said, with a smile.

"You are an amazing woman," I said.

"Come on, let's get out of here and have a drink," she said.

On the street, she walked beside me with her arm in mine. It was almost dark, a frigid wind blowing down the avenue.

"Do you want to get a cab? You definitely deserve one," I said.

"Let's take subway. I'm changing my life."

On the way uptown she talked excitedly about the interview.

"Dr. Valdes is a whopper — you know — big and fat! She is only my psychiatrist. They assign me to therapist. I go to therapist twice a week. And see Dr. Valdes when therapist thinks necessary. And she gave me prescription."

"That's great!"

"So, are you happy?"

"I'm fabulously proud of you," I said.

"Hmm."

I put my arms around her.

"You know — *proud*?"

In one of her letters, she writes:

> I want to be with you
> and I want to be able
>   to LOVE
> even if it will take hours
> to come to understanding
> I wouldn't trade it for a
> fleeting second of false
>   happiness.

From the beginning Irina's therapist — a woman whose initials happened to be H.D. — seeded the thought in Irina's mind that by helping her write I was attempting to control her.

"What did she say?" I asked.

"She said that I don't need anyone to help me write my poems," Irina explained.

It was devastating, nightmarish, after the traumatic weeks it had taken to convince her to do this.

"Oh, God!" I said. "She doesn't know what she's talking about." I had a sense of drowning. "She thinks I'm . . . how about translating Pasternak? Does she want you to do that by yourself too?"

"Well . . . she said, why does he want you to do, if it's already been done?"

"We have to find somebody else for you to see," I said.

"I'm not going to change therapists," she said, with blind allegiance.

"But she's wrong!" I was furious. "She's the wrong person. She's turning you against me. Irina, you need someone you can really talk to, not some bitter, nattering idiot planting things in your mind!"

"I can have my own thoughts. She explained it. She is only there to guide me. When I get off subject she helps me come back. I'm working with her on issues — you know, issues?"

"What about your medication?" I asked.

"She's not sure I need it. I told her you want me to take it. You know what she said? Pretty soon he'll have you in nut-house."

She had taken her medication for a couple of weeks, and then quit. "All it does is give you a little time to think before you act — one tiny millisecond when I'm going out door at three in the morning. That's all."

H.D., the real one, the poet courted in a tree by the sixteen-year-old Ezra Pound — "Dryad" of the *Cantos* and author of *Helen in Egypt* — had visions. Images appeared on a wall in Corfu. She was an analysand of Freud's. She wrote: "There is no great art period without great lovers."

———

After every therapy session Irina is remote and cold, dissoci-
ating herself from understandings that existed between us the
day before. The therapist, she explains, has clarified our relationship for her. "It's not about love, it's about *codependency*.
And *neediness*," she says. "I have to found myself to be free. I
talked to her about that 'surrender' — I was kind fascinated.
You know what she said: it is form of subjugation."

We had gone roller-blading and were sitting on a bench in
Battery Park City.

"I would like to meet with her," I said.

"You don't know about therapy. You've never even been to
therapist," she said.

"I want us to see her together."

"Maybe later. Not now," she said. "You're not my father."

Near where we sat were the lines of poetry by Whitman
and Frank O'Hara, inset in the black railing at the edge of the
river. Blinding sunlight balanced on the water's undulations.

"Let's make a lobster salad for dinner," I said.

She didn't respond, and turned away.

"What's the matter? Don't you like lobster salad?"

"I'm going home," she said in a dead tone.

The sudden, truculent despair left a pantomime of help-
lessness in its wake.

"What's wrong? We were having such a nice day skating.
What is it?"

"I feel manipulated," she said.

"What do you mean?"

"I'm going home."

She got up and started to walk away. When I tried to stop
her, to talk to her, she jerked her arm free.

"Leave me alone! Let me go! Don't touch me!"

I said, "Just tell me what's wrong, what made you feel manipulated."

"I listen to my heart!" she hissed through her teeth. "My heart never lies to me!"

Locked in resentment, in its terrible cell. *He wants to make a lobster salad; he wants to fuck me; everybody wants to fuck me; I despise all of them; I dance naked and piss in their lobster salad.* In my own behavior, when I can't return to the surface, I know it. I'm aware that Irina is being sacrificed for my ignoble paralysis; disgusted with myself, I push through and try, stumblingly, to right things. With Irina no light gets in, no release is possible. The incident is crumpled in her brain. Every imagined manipulation is perceived as an attempt to take sexual advantage. Her fears reveal her, the terms that warrant her presence in anybody's bed; that, and the failure to know now, in the dim lamp of therapy, what we had on our own at least marked as a signpost before: that lovers give themselves to each other.

Wanting to be with Irina was like the pursuit of a goddess. All contact was subject to favor — spun out of her own unpredictable desires — indifference, or scorn. When we met at the movies or the museum, when she walked into a restaurant, dazzling and late, these were the moods I danced around. Her hand, if I held it, withdrew, eluding the compact. I wanted her to be human. Anyone less willing to frame his hopes in flames might simply have stopped. My needs, limits, damages, and strengths were not just exposed but revealed in an unexpected relation. Yet her life opened into mine; the outlines of her talent, greater than my own, grew visible. The first steps toward trust, tenderness itself — caught and quickly smothered against her breast — were glimpsed again and again in the interstices of our days and nights. You close the door and the world is inside. I loved her tortured hair, the helix of her ear, the wide bowl of her hips, her body, her body, the beanie flamingos in her brain. I was easily hurt and tormented by feelings of rejection and jealousy. But the pain — I touch her back and feel her pull away — floats beside us. We inhabit a relative universe, a landscape of desire, in which bizarre and insurmountable difficulties are its common horizon.

Through the painted scrim, we see what he cannot: she doesn't love him is all. But that wasn't it. The demarcation won't convert to a declarative structure. We were a part of contrary currents, their irresolution doubling what it meant to want her — and what wanting her meant. Happiness — when it was there — was incontestable; yet our lives were like a series of discrete, self-consuming incidents. Mortgaged to an inexhaustible negative. You cannot stop, you can only fail.

Everything is as far away as it can be — and then folded into the translation. The unattainable is its principle.

Dear *Elvira*,
The moment I start to speak, you stand there, a six-year-old child with your hands over your ears. You are like the evil dwarf who will disappear forever if someone guesses her name. And you are furious and frightened that I have discovered it.

I'm addressing you instead of Irina because I realize now that you are the one who has the power. I can talk to Irina about you, you permit our conversations, and it gives Irina the illusion of freedom. But you know perfectly well that she has none. Your control is unremitting. Any time your dominance is threatened, you swiftly intervene, the hideous face behind the painted mask.

You can fool Irina and confuse her, but you can't fool

me. Your primary aim is to ensure her unhappiness. Only
in that is the punishment of your parents and brother
accomplished. No matter what I say to Irina to combat
this, you white it out in her mind. Because *if Irina were
happy, you would cease to exist.*

A writer friend of mine saw us one night at a restaurant and
called me the next day. "I understand," he said, an arrogant
swagger in his voice. "I've gone out with women who look like
that. It's better than having a Porsche." When she thought
about her looks (she didn't always; her mind, if it was clear, was
like a pair of hands with a single thing clasped tightly in one
and in the other — surprise! — nothing), it was as if an anger
had been abruptly remembered. The idea of herself as beautiful — its presence in her consciousness — unleashed the paranoia she brought to any potential intimacy. Seeing only a shallow, vain (and divine) apparition in the horror of her mirror, she
projected the same mentality onto every attention she received.
She was a tower girl, like Herodiade, standing at the barred window with fierce eyes. An allure reigned, defying any lover not to
be overcome by its perfection — and therefore despised.

In a small, whining voice, she said, "Can you come?"
    "What's wrong?" I asked.
    Her body continued to move with mine.
    "I want you to hurry up."
    "We . . . just started," I breathed.
    "I want you to come!" The whine in her voice rose, she was
almost whimpering. "I don't want to do this now!"
    She didn't stop. To help, to hurry me she increased the
intensity of our movements to a climactic rush.
    I came almost at once in deep violent strokes and lay

shuddering in her arms. She held me for a moment, and then began to struggle impatiently. I pulled out of her, my penis thick and still half-erect. She turned over and curled up on the far side of the bed.

"What is it?" I said.

She didn't answer.

"Irina, what happened?"

"I just don't feel like it!" she said in a muffled voice.

"You did a minute ago," I said.

"Well, I don't now!" she shouted.

I sighed, and lay down beside her. Without touching her breasts, I slipped my arm around her waist.

Later, we woke up and got under the covers. Her face was angelic from the innocence of sleep. She snuggled close to me and kissed me good-night, her smile half-awake, tender and infinitely sweet.

A day or two before my play opened, we made plans to meet at the theater. "Let's say seven o'clock, O.K.?" she suggested. "That way I'll be there by eight." During the weeks of rewriting and rehearsals, Irina had barely conceded its existence. But now she was conscious of it as an occasion.

"I don't know what I'm going to wear," she said. "Maybe costume!"

The lobby was small, hung with head-shots of the actors and posters from previous shows. The audience, chiefly pals and supporters of the cast, began to arrive. Friends wished me well, the glitter of excitement in their voices. It was a modest production. Still, whatever its value, the event itself — a show opening in New York — was charged with a momentary exhilaration. I looked forward to seeing my play come to life, but with an attention divided, anchored in the idea of sitting beside her in the dark theater with the words and music I had

written, if they happened to please, becoming a further increment in the critical mass of our lives. I would have liked for
her to be proud of me; but more, for pride, in its little wind, to
be a flag of our sovereignty. The houselights blinked for the
second time. Irina was late. I waited until the last minute and
then, as the performance started, took a seat at the back of the
theater. I watched the fizzy lightness of the first scenes with
a distracted heart, the movement and bright colors. Halfway
through the act Irina arrived, accompanied by a woman I didn't
recognize, and was seated in the front row. We met after the
performance in the lobby. People were milling around, talking
about the play, some offering congratulations.

"This is my friend Ilse from Prague," said Irina, manic and
bubbly. "We've been shopping and drinking — and drinking
and shopping. We haven't met until this afternoon, but now
we old friends. Tonight is her last days in New York. She has
to run to catch plane."

Ilse was tall and thin with a poor complexion and frowsy,
light brown hair.

"It was nice," she murmured with a slight accent, and kissed
Irina good-bye.

My friend who had put the production together said that
one of the producers he'd invited was interested in talking to
us and would be at the party afterward.

Irina said, "Oh, do we have to go to party?"

"We don't have to, but we probably should," I said.

"I'm not feeling very well," she said.

"We won't stay long," I said.

"I just want to have quiet dinner. You go."

"I don't want to go without you."

"I don't feel like being with all these people — you know,
theater people."

"O.K., we won't go," I said.

"Are you sure?"

"Yes. So, where would you like to eat?"

"I don't know. Some place we can have glass of wine. Maybe uptown around Lincoln Center. Or somewhere else."

We got a cab on Broadway. It had begun to drizzle; droplets skidded on the windows, each holding a dazzle, as we drove through the city. I knew that my actions were foolhardy and irresponsible. Like a gambler who consecrates his ruin to the fates, I was in over my head. The question of why produced only an answering etiology, a map of who I was.

The play had a short run and closed without Irina returning to see it.

Her moral absence, if that is what it was — the failure to imagine love — appeared on the screen of my perceptions as a series of betrayals and rejections. Emotions, orchestrated by a beautiful, vampy stranger, maintained a complex chase of erotic cognates through every dimension of our lives. And love, passing through the eye of the same needle, with the wild certainty of its power, night after night held in its arms only a simulacrum. I couldn't fuck her enough. She was gone through the looking glass. It was always only sex; nothing else was touched, nothing altered by the profound act.

We had a toehold — in poetry, in the Pasternak translations, with our lives scribbled like children's drawings in the margins. A center endured. "There are rocks that don't move," Irina insisted. To face the horror of bad days, to supplant them with better ones, was a position of trust. The phone would ring; the air of clotted anguish would seep back into the night before. "There is no one I want to see or be with but you."

We went to Port Jefferson one afternoon to ride the ferry from the North Shore of Long Island across the Sound. When we got there it was too late to make the crossing over and back in the daylight, which was what Irina wanted to do.

"Let's stay here," she said, "and go tomorrow. I love taking ferry."

We found a motel, a row of gray-shingled cottages, down near the wharf. In a grocery store she bought beer, wine, and a toothbrush.

"It will be like excursion," she said.

In the warm, leafy afternoon we wandered with gratuitous leisure through the town, her mind clear and calm.

"Have you ever heard of this — an oxygen parlor?"

She looked in the window.

"The walls are peach!" she said, and sneezed.

Later, we had dinner in a large restaurant overlooking the harbor, and then walked back to the motel, crickets and frogs scoring the dark.

She poured a glass of wine and sat in one of the kitchen chairs, searching around in her purse.

"This is poem I wrote in Russia when I was eighteen," she said. "Can you imagine?"

"Is it in English?"

"No, Russian. You want to hear it anyway?"

"Sure," I said.

"Well . . ."

She crossed her legs and smiled at me. Her hair, burnished by the spill of lamplight, was pushed back from her forehead in a gentle wave. As she read I could hear the Russian rhymes tumbling over each other. The poem sounded like a short ballad. The clear pitch of her voice, slightly formalized in the precision of her delivery, hung in the air. I was never far from an awareness that this phenomenal person, with her strange songs, had become a part of my everyday life. "I wrote tons of poems in Russia. Everybody does. We could try to translate one, if you like to," she said. And then added exuberantly, "Why not, it might be fun, who cares, I didn't know what I was doing."

In English, the poem turned out to be dense, ungraspable, its images packed together like a Russian doll. There was no air, no connective tissue, and yet the images by themselves were wonderful. I puzzled over it for an hour or so. Irina's mood was warm and serene. In a white tank top, she sat propped up in bed reading the *Times*, the beautiful shape of a leg escaping from loose khaki shorts.

"Don't worry about it — I like what I write in English better. Come to bed. Or just fix it. Do whatever. It's not big deal. Have a beer." She went into the kitchen and came back with a beer.

"You're all image," I said.

"You're all action," she said.

Later, while she was in the shower, I wrote a series of small riffs, using as touchpoints the images in her poem. Interlinear, half-serious, they were improvisations that played to the strengths that were there, adding breathing room and a conversational tone.

"What are you doing?" she said. "Ooh, that light is too bright." She got into bed, her eyes shy without makeup, ducking under the sheet.

I sat up, with Irina dozing beside me, and completed what was less a translation than an extended duet. Only poems love poems. The title of my version referred in part to the process of its making, but more to the transformation in Irina that we both hoped was an actuality.

The Conversion of Elvira

1.

I make the long trip back in the blue
of your eyes and I'm smiling. How

did I get here on this weightless raft
of heaven, so far from that river
where only a second ago the barge haulers
were droning and dragging me down?

2.
Such excessive weight,
the lure sinks
straight to the bottom. It's not
inventive — you know, *inventive*?
Anyway, this is the Lake
of Temptation, cypresses
stand in the yellow water
up to their waists. The taut black line
snags on something. Who knows
what's at this end, much less
at the other. The empty
treasure chest of conscience. All
the trout swim away. I really should
get some sleep now.
In the morning we'll unpack
the luggage of the past.

3.
If he's angry that's one thing,
but this is too gloomy. It unravels —
with, write, lisp, fright, writhe.
Fear, like a pilgrim of solitary nights
(who is imaginary in my mind
but not in yours), slips into the huge
house and begins to bellow.
Call that an impetuous gesture.
And before, when the heavy
helmet fell to the ground
a flock of rooks rose up.

4.
It was inevitable but shouldn't
have happened — like L.A.
Slyness coats the blue pill
of sky. Not forgetting
about daffodils is different
than believing in them. The
piano plays in the smoke-filled
past of two people. One
is always you, the other
purely an imagined state,
like the happiness of bees.

5.
(They won't dissolve
or ever drown wearing
those colorful life-rings
around them in the water.)

6.
Sleep's hard to know about. You're
asleep. The in-between surfaces
flourish in slack contrast. Put
that sofa over there. Aside from
mortal bliss, I wish I knew
what she meant. It was arranged
in stacks of lumber, their bodies
rotate emitting a strange
damp odor, maybe beer, in
the room's pure shimmer, the
length of shadow, the cooling
pulse of not just anyone's.

. . . .

Let
let the rain
let the rain paint
let the rain paint the window.

It's chilly in the bright haze, crossing the Sound. We find a spot out of the wind, the sunlight on the water bronze and warming, the rhythmic lull of the ferry's engines. She has on a pink and turquoise T-shirt, one she wore on our first trip. I know her clothes, the morning recital of her dreams. Behind dark glasses, her eyes are suffused, staring out over the glittering water. The wind moves her hair. Lazily, with her head propped on one hand, she turns toward me, and smiles.

Walking up from the harbor, we pass a house that has at the front of a wide lawn an iron gate. No fence, just the gate standing alone, stoically closed against intruders. It catches Irina's eye, the absurdity of it. Laughing, she marches onto the lawn and strikes a pose behind the gate, one foot raised up to the top of the gatepost — as if she were trapped and trying to climb out.

three

It had snowed all day, light and lingering in the still air. I heard the chime of the elevator as it stopped on my floor, like a Russian bell tinkling in blue distances. Heels struck the landing in quick succession, followed by the sound of the buzzer. She had her own key, but never used it.

"Oof! It's beautiful out — still snowing — but do you like my boots?"

She pointed the toe of a high black boot at me. Tightly knit laces ran up the side, the length of her calf.

"I'll never get you out of those," I said.

"They zeep," she said.

She handed me an armful of flowers, white chrysanthemums and bird-of-paradise, wrapped in deli-paper.

"I'm late — I know," she said, taking off her coat. "I'm going to be better. O.K. — we go to movie tomorrow, I promise."

She stepped out of her boots, walking on her toes.

"Here — I'll do it," she said, carrying the flowers into the kitchen. "The Koreans has nothing very good."

I stood behind her at the sink with my arms around her. I kissed the back of her neck, and brushed in soft valediction the nipple of a breast.

"I had vision tonight — I guess you'd say," she said.

"What was it?"

"I was walking near my apartment, on sidewalk. I looked up and saw the sun. It was like bright ball of yarn in the sky."

"But the sky was dark."

"Yes."

"So, what happened?"

"It was ball of yellow yarn, and there was one strand hanging down sort of teasing me to go with it — you know? — to follow it somewhere."

"Like where?"

"I have no idea. But I thought — this is vision. I wasn't scared."

The flowers lay in the sink, under the splattering tap.

"When did this happen?" I asked.

"Just now, when I was coming over here. That's it!" she suddenly laughed, making the association. "It was telling me hurry up."

Immediately she turned it into a riff, speaking in the sun's voice.

"You are late! Hurry up! Go to movie!"

She put the flowers in a blue-speckled enamel pitcher and set them on the kitchen table. I remained standing by the sink. She walked back to where I was, and stopped, letting her body fall forward into mine.

After "Frost," we decided to translate a spring poem called "Wind" — chosen as a declaration that we would be together through another season.

"I think this is poem about Pasternak's mistress," Irina said. "She was much younger, and was arrested — you know — imprisoned."

Wind

I'm finished, but you're alive,
and the crying, complaining wind
rocks the forest and the dacha.
Not each pine separately
but with infinite distance
all the trees together,

like the hull of a sailboat
on the mirrory surface of a bay.
This isn't due to daring
or from aimless rage
but in sadness to find for you
the words of a lullaby.

"The Russian word is *toska*," Irina explained. "It means sadness, but much deeper than the sadness of English."

"Sorrow?"

"No, it's not sentimental. It's heroic, a national mood. This word is very Russian. They great! Snow and destiny and toska!"

She took a sip of beer, swishing it into fizz in her mouth, giggling.

I made it a point not to read any English versions of the poems we were translating. Yet shortly after we finished working on "Hops" — also set in spring — I remembered it was one of the poems Robert Lowell had translated with Olga Carlisle, in *Imitations*. One night in a bookstore I decided to take a look at it. I knew that Lowell had treated the originals as springboards for his improvisations, but I was still curious to see what relation ours might have with that of the legendary poet's. I found the poem and read the first two lines.

Lowell:

Beneath a willow entwined with ivy,
we look for shelter from the bad weather.

Us:

Beneath the ivy-entwined willow,
we found shelter from the wet weather.

Lowell retitles the poem "Wild Vines" and, as the poem progresses, adds a number of words and phrases that are not in the original. But in the beginning lines, where no liberties have been taken, it was heartening to see how closely our versions matched. Not so much for stylistic reasons, but for a corroboration of content. The sibyl-like magic at midnight worked. I even felt that Lowell's use of "look for" instead of "found" was slightly imprecise.

It is a poem about a couple making love. They become intoxicated with each other, and the raincoat winds up under them, spread out on the ground. I made a little broadside of the poem, with a pencil drawing of a raincoat as an illustration. For the lining, peeking out from its loose folds, I painted a field of white daisies with yellow centers floating on a blue ground.

Irina is reading Eliot's *Four Quartets*. The train pulls out of the city. It is a freezing gray day in early spring. Pigeons huddled on narrow ledges are edged off into the air by sleet-filled gusts of wind. They blow like rags in the sky. I'm reading Yeats's strange book *A Vision*. The fields we pass are covered with deep, bone-gray snow. Irina is focused, calm, her face softened by the pewter afternoon light. Destructive impulses that thrive in her everyday life are almost absent on our trips. Only we inhabit the moving moment. The whistle will sound. The whistle sounds. Soon (we are tunneling through a corridor of evergreens) she'll turn with bright, child-like excitement and say: "Listen to this: *'A raid on the inarticulate!'*"

Then — and now — I listen.

Coming into Baltimore, we're eating peanut butter sandwiches.

"How is your book?" she asks.

"I thought I might find out something about visions," I say.

"Did you?"

"Not yet."

She picks it up and flips through it, glancing at a few of the diagrams. She makes a face and hands it back.

"You're probably right," I say. "It came about because Yeats's wife was involved in automatic writing. They were supposedly in contact with some kind of otherworldly sources who were dictating to them."

"My friend Otto knows about automatic writing. So, they did this — Yeats and his wife?" she asks.

"Well, according to Yeats, that's what happened. They were living in Rapallo at the time. Pound was also living there. At one point, he wrote a letter to somebody — I can't remember who — in which he referred to things at chez Yeats as 'Very, very, very bughouse.'"

Trust is a part of the overnight bag that she carefully packs for our trips. She is warm and vibrant, connected to clear depths. This is who I believe her to be.

"Did we bring the wine?" she asks.

"Yes, do you want some now?"

"What kind is it?"

"Red."

"I think I'll have an apple. I want to read a little more of this." She laughs. "I don't know what hell he is talking about half time, but it's wonderful. This book is just what I need!"

From the train station, we take the Washington subway, with its clean, quiet cars, to DuPont Circle, and then walk through bitter cold to the hotel. A pinion fire burns in the bar, which is furnished with overstuffed couches and lamps with painted shades. Generous stairways carpeted with worn floral patterns lead up to the rooms. Our room has a white brass bed, Oriental rugs, ceiling fans, a Japanese screen with scarlet parrots. We make love almost immediately on the unturned-down bed, and again, in the large, lion-footed bathtub, folded intricately into the lubricious water, which grows finally cool around our bodies.

Tall townhouse windows face onto the snowy street. The restaurant in the hotel is closed when we come downstairs. We take a cab to the Washington Mall. Stars glitter in the dark between low moving clouds.

After a late Chinese dinner, Irina says, "Let's explore a little while." She looks suddenly willful. "I want to see this Lincoln Abraham guy!"

Aside from an officer in a small guardhouse, we're the only people at the Lincoln Memorial. Irina reads the texts on the walls. "This is on my test — what I have to know for citizenship," she says.

We walk up the Mall, through a lunar field of frozen snow, to the Vietnam Veterans Memorial. There are flowers here and there placed against the wall. We can see our reflections, our breath against the black writing. It's tremendously cold.

"Let's start back — do you want to?" I say.

She rubs friction hands over my coat to warm me.

"Good idea," she says.

There is very little traffic. A cab passes on the opposite side of the boulevard, but doesn't respond to us. We wait for another one. Five or ten minutes go by. Irina holds my arm with both hands, hiding her face from the wind. I spot the lit medallion of a cab and sprint to the corner, getting there just as the cab starts to pull away. He has a fare in the backseat.

"Can you call and get a cab to pick us up?" I ask the driver.

"It wouldn't do any good — too late, too cold. You better take the subway," he says.

The subway, it turns out, is closed for the night by the time we get to the nearest station. We start walking in the direction of the hotel. In heels, in the freezing, wind-bitten night, Irina doesn't once complain.

"It's like Moscow — only Moscow is much worse. You should see it, oh, my God! This is April in Moscow! You know — an April day?"

It takes us an hour to get back to the hotel. In our room, Irina lights a candle she brought with us. We drink a glass of wine and go to bed. The windows are streaked with ice. Under the covers, our bodies touch without self-consciousness, exhausted. Her breasts flatten against my chest as she turns and kisses me good-night.

"This was wonderful trip," she says. "Thank you for bringing me."

It is silent outside — a pristine clarity of cold — calm and surrounding. I lie in the dark, her breath faintly felt on my shoulder. Our nights are rarely this free of tension, the unison of mood rarely so simply shared. The bottom of her foot rests on the top of mine. The smallest movement is a frictional spark, a caress to extend and sustain the flood of well-being. I turn and kiss the stillness of her face, half asleep. It is an act that carries with it a tinge of the apprehension that vibrates through our lives. At any moment the reversal could occur. She pushes closer to me, her mouth moving across my cheek like a drowsy moth. Her legs swim into mine. We make love slowly, the tiredness of our bodies leisurely disappearing. Her skin is moist with sweat, the covers tumble off onto the floor. A luminosity glazes her body. To hold on to this moment, to perpetuate with indelible passion its place in our lives, against opacity and the return of distortion, is a desire that is folded into the intoxication of sex, an overreaching depth, wet on wet, of which ecstasy is the breaking wave.

In the morning, bright sunlight wakes us, filling the room over the low buildings. She gets out of bed and walks naked into the bathroom, her toes curling up over the thick rug. Her face is unguarded, sleep-swollen, beautiful.

"Give me twenty minutes," she says.

We have eggs and croissants downstairs in the hotel. A thin blond woman and a senator are seated a few tables away. After breakfast we take the subway to the museum. Vermeer's masterpiece, *The Art of Painting*, on loan from Vienna, is installed in a small show at the National Gallery, along with the four Vermeers in the permanent collection.

"This is what we came to see," I say.

She stands self-forgetful for a moment, looking at the girl in the blue dress, who poses with a yellow book and brass trumpet. On the wall between the pulled-back curtain and the map, a silver blade of light points upward. The artist himself, his girth a solid volume, sits with his back to the viewer in the tiled room, painting the laurel leaves in the muse's hair.

I spent the early part of the evening working on a Pasternak poem. We had done the first drafts of several poems, including "Silence," "Winter Nights," and "Explanation," with its lines that sounded like they were about us.

> . . . We are bare wires.
> Any moment could throw us
> Into each other.

We met for dinner in a restaurant in the neighborhood, and afterwards went for a walk in the park. New snow had fallen over the hard, lumpy ground. At one point she slipped. When I tried to take her arm she moved away.

"What's the matter?" I said.

We had just recently come back from the sweet, sane days of Washington. (Happiness was revoked for the offense of having existed.)

"I'm not staying at your apartment tonight," she said with sudden defiance.

"O.K., that's fine," I said.

I looked out over the snow. The park was immaculate,

a grisaille of ivory, lit by the low aurora of clouds. Close to where we were standing, there was a rip the size of a small window, near the top of the chain-link fence that surrounded the Central Park reservoir. Through it, you could see unobstructed the flat expanse of flawless snow, spread out over the ice. A great luminous disk.

"Look at this," I said.

She didn't answer.

"It's very beautiful."

"I can see it," she said.

"I mean from here, without the fence in front of it," I said.

"No."

She was standing a few feet away.

"You won't come over here and look at it?"

"No."

"God, you're exasperating!" I said.

She turned and walked away, back toward the street. I followed ponderously behind her.

"You know what we're like?" I said.

She looked toward the approaching traffic for a cab.

"We're like a comic opera. One of us is a fragile man-boy who flies into quixotic postures of defense at every imagined slight."

Her eyes are stony, unyielding.

"But," I said, "this is because he believes that his love for . . . the other person in the opera . . . is pure and ethical."

I kiss her on the cheek.

"Don't do that!" She moves away from me.

"The other person in the opera — whom he really does love, as a matter of fact — is a mad child woman whose mind interprets all his attentions as simply a deceitful manipulation to try to fuck her."

"You don't know anything about opera," she sneered.

A cab pulled to a stop beside her.

"Don't run away. This is exactly when we ought to try to talk," I said.

"I'm going home." She got into the cab and left.

I walked along the edge of the park for a while and then back to my apartment. At my desk I read through the most recent of the Pasternak poems we had worked on.

Rendezvous

The roads are covered with snow,
the rooftops piled high.
To stretch my legs I go
out the door you're standing by.

In a fall coat, alone,
without galoshes or hat,
you struggle with emotion,
crumbs of snow wet

on your lips. Into mist, all
the fences and trees disappear.
You stand in snowfall
alone on the corner.

Water runs from the scarf
down your sleeve where,
like dew, it soaks the cuff.
It glistens in your hair.

The blond hair
illuminates with one lock
the face, scarf, figure,
and the shabby frock.

Your look is
all of a piece — snow

on your eyelashes,
in your eyes, sorrow.

The image of your life
is etched with the art
of an invisible knife
upon my heart.

The humility of your features
lodged forever in it —
that's why the indifference
of the world's irrelevant.

And that's why I'm your
double. In the borderless
night, the lines blur
that would divide us.

And who are we,
after years, and from where,
if rumors remain,
but we're not there?

The following night she arrived and referred only casually
to the fact that she hadn't felt well the previous evening. "My
stomach is little funny."

I didn't say anything.

"Did you have a good day? I'm happy to see you," she said.

"I'm happy to see you too," I said, halfheartedly.

She ignored my reticence.

"Oh, I want to show you these — O.K.? They have lots of
problems, I think." Her voice remained upbeat as she handed
me a folder. "I want to know what you think. I've been writing
lot lately."

"But what if tomorrow you come back from therapy and
start telling me that I'm trying to control you?"

"Oh, come on! Don't worry, I'm completely present," she said, with a pleading smile.

Her attempts to disavow or downplay the existence of other behaviors were always successful, mainly because I didn't want to destroy the moments that were good. I continued to believe in their ascendancy.

"Just look at one," she laughed and blew in my ear.

Translating Pasternak was a project between lovers; it was fun, and valuable to her self-esteem. Her own poems were vital to her identity. They were the enactments of a struggle to make sense. Ironically, as a poet, this was the one thing she couldn't do. It was also the least important. Each of Irina's poems rose with feral strength out of depths she herself could scarcely guess at — an animal with her arms around it. I knew their lacks and flaws only because I knew so intimately and respectfully the ways they were virtuous. I was astonished by and proud of her talent. In Yeats's line, I was prepared "to spend what remained of life" helping her with them. Language is a way of behaving; missteps in writing are lived moments. She got lost in the details of her poems, in the musculature of their intentions. I could trace in their extraordinary lines the confusion, the hiatus of thought that left her stranded. An objective correlative existed in the poem itself. Naively perhaps, I believed that in its concrete order she could encounter and change herself, through powers she possessed as a poet. Every writer knows that syllables have saved his life.

We drank beer and made love on the couch.

As the weather turned warm, the cherry trees and white plums bloomed in the park. The handful of irresolute New York days that pass for spring dissolved into premature summer. Irina found a part-time job, through a woman who lived in my building, with a company in Chelsea that made costumes and scenery for the theater. She was taking her medication.

Our lives were not significantly different, but descents into hell were mixed with mysterious algorithms of success. Her job was the dark stranger at the door; it represented, like every encounter in her history, the potential to separate herself from her present circumstances. I could feel it like a wind blowing through our lives. But she was also proud of her accomplishment and excited by its newness.

"I would never done this, if it hadn't been for you," she said.

"I didn't do it — you did it," I said.

"*We* did," she said. "They like having me around — you know, around? I can arrange my own hours. They call me when they need extra help. Somebody is there even at one in morning. They all gay. They smart — you know — because they understand women. I think I'm gay too. We're making feathers — hundreds of lavender feathers. I can do faster than the guy who taught me. He's been there three years. Can you imagine — three *years*!"

She went with me on a weekend trip to Tucson, where I gave a lecture and poetry reading at the University of Arizona. While we were there we drove down to Nogales, through the quiet desert landscape, its silver grays and greens "grateful to the eye," as Mary Austin wrote.

"Let's buy hammock," Irina said.

We crossed the border into Mexico on foot and wandered around the town of brightly colored houses, dirt streets, and bony roaming dogs. At one side of the town, a white concrete stairway led in successive flights up a high, steep embankment. Irina went ahead of me, glancing back at each landing, her face in dark glasses framed against the blue sky and brilliant angles of white. From the top, we could see the entire town, the bare surrounding hills. A small band was playing in the plaza, with people dancing.

"Look at my panties," Irina said, lifting her skirt up like a little girl.

They were a thin-winged V of see-through material, fuchsia,

with opaque patterns outlined in gold thread. I ran my fingers over the silken fabric, pressing upward into her.

"You're beautiful," I said. I pulled her close to me, with my hand tucked into the back of her panties, my finger in the cleft of her ass. The sun was intense, high overhead in the silent day, like a tent of brightness.

"Let's do it," I said.

"You crazy!" she said.

I walked her backwards into the whitewashed wall at the top of the stairs.

"We can see anyone who starts to come up," I said, kissing her neck.

"What about those," she said.

A few houses were perched behind us along the edge of the cliff.

"Everyone's in town," I said.

I kissed her again, pressing my erection against her. Her body pushed into mine; with swept-away urgency, her hands circled my neck.

A large dun-colored dog came around the corner of one of the houses, along a path leading to the stairs, followed by an elderly woman with a stick. As they passed us the woman smiled and said, "Buenas tardes."

"You are crazyman," Irina said, laughing. "Let's go find hammock."

We wandered through the mercado, where she picked out a hammock of blue and green webbing, and then walked back to the border.

The immigration official was a fat Mexican-American, with an unlit cigar in his mouth and a gold tooth.

"American citizen?" he asked, perfunctorily, as we passed through.

"Yes," I said.

"Anything to declare?"

"Just this hammock."

"How much did you pay for it?"

"Twenty dollars."

"O.K., go through."

"Well . . . actually I'm Russian citizen," Irina said.

"Do you have a green card?" he asked.

"I do," she said, "but it's in New York."

"You have to have it with you," he said.

Irina was immediately flustered and on the defensive.

"I didn't know I'm going to Mexico? He should have told me." Then to me she said, "It's always better to tell truth."

"What do we have to do?" I asked.

"The fine's a hundred and seventy dollars," he said.

"Isn't there a way to verify that she has a green card — a computer check or something?" I asked.

"Yeah!" he said insolently, "and if she's got one, you can pay the fine and take her home with you."

Irina looked like an exotic bird, lost and scared.

"I need to go to an ATM," I said.

"On the American side, in town," he pointed. "She stays here."

Another official was called to escort Irina to a nearby building.

"I'll be right back," I said. "Don't worry."

I jogged the ten or twelve blocks into town along a dusty road. The balance in my account was $418.00. When I returned Irina was casually smoking a cigarette, surrounded by three or four swarthy border-patrol cops. As I came in she laughed and said, "It's all *his* fault."

We drove back to Tucson with the sun setting, the long shadows of giant saguaros like cartoons. "Well," Irina said, "we bought most expensive hammock in whole goddamn of Mexico."

The night before we left, Kathleen, the young woman who

ran the lecture program at the university, stopped by to ask me to sign the guest book, which belonged to the cottage where we had stayed. I introduced her to Irina as I glanced at the recent signatures of visiting authors.

"Are you also a poet?" Kathleen asked.

"Well . . . I don't know . . . I'm trying to work on . . ."

"She is *definitely* a poet," I said.

"Oh, then please — sign the guest book," said Kathleen.

One night I proposed that we pick out a few of Irina's best poems and try to get them published. The next day she brought over a manuscript for me to look through. At this point, I was also working on various art projects, trying to find enough money to keep us going. I was paying her rent and for her therapy. The following night, at one-thirty in the morning, she called just as I was falling asleep.

"I was wondering about, did you send my poems to *New Yorker*?"

"Not yet," I mumbled.

A stark silence.

"Irina . . ."

No answer.

"Irina, are you there?" I asked.

No answer.

"Talk to me . . . what's wrong?" I said.

"It's just exactly what I know — you're trying to control me," she said.

"Oh, God . . . please don't start that. You must have gone to therapy today. I haven't had time to look at the poems. I'll do it tomorrow. We can do it together."

"*No!*" The voice of a six-year-old.

"Don't," I pleaded.

"You didn't send them and you said you would."

"It's only been a day."

"It's been two days."

"I'm sorry, I'm half asleep. I'll call you tomorrow. Everything'll be fine, don't worry." I said.

"We're finished — don't call me again," she said.

"Stop. We've been doing so well lately. We're translating Pasternak, we're working on your poems. I just got busy with things I had to do. I love you. Go to sleep and we'll talk tomorrow."

"You're using my poetry to get me into your bed," she said.

"Irina, you've been in my bed for ten months," I said.

"You're using me! I don't accept it! I have my rights!" she hollered.

The irrational element that permeates these exchanges unweights them and gives to your own responses a slightly inauthentic aura, an absence of pathways.

"Irina, listen — I'm trying to make money so that you . . ."

"I'm not listening to you," she said.

". . . so that you don't have to think about . . ."

"I'm not listening, I'm not listening."

". . . so that you don't have to . . ."

"I'm not listening."

"Please stop interrupting and let me . . ."

"I'm not listening to you. I'm not listening."

"Let me speak — please!"

"I'm not listening I'm not listening I'm not listening . . ."

I said: "Pick up your poems, Irina. I'll leave them with the doorman."

I knew, even before I said it, I was engaging in an empty gesture; it was something numbly opted for, since nothing else had any effect. I hung up the phone, furious at the situation, the nightmare recurrence of being trapped in a zone where nothing counts — and where a cheap tactic acted out against an unbalanced mind had become an option. I got out of bed, dressed, and stuck her poems in an envelope to leave with the doorman downstairs — aware of the charade I was performing, ashamed, and knowing that if I thought twice about it I'd change my mind. On the other hand, it was a decisive act with its own unsheathed anger. At two in the morning, in the small life of its momentum, it was a symbolic act against months and months of frustration. I thought about her Russian-English dictionary sitting on the windowsill in the kitchen, so carefully not gathered up and removed with her notebook and other things at the end of the evening. I went back and looked at it. It was a luminous object. I took it with me.

From the beginning Irina was, in kaleidoscopic permutations, a singular stress. A system of self-defeat tugged against its anchor. I refuted delusions, tamed fears, countered the logic of negation, rebuilt every day the ruined city of love, picked her up, held her in arms determined to outlast the force of her opposition. Suddenly the tension changed, went slack, aggressively reversed itself. She toppled backwards. What for other couples would have been no more than a fight, put back together the next day, was for Irina the end. She was a fury of confusion and hurt. Talking was impossible. She was completely unequipped to negotiate even the simplest resolution. She wanted us to talk, but each time we tried she would rage incoherently, never allowing me to speak, and then storm away. She treated all my attempts to persuade her that we should be together again as manipulations to get her back into bed.

"No sex," she said.

We were sitting in Riverside Park, not far from where she first showed me her poems. On the river a small white sail passed slowly into the distance, like a mute proclamation delivered to the trees.

Irina said, "I'm not going to have sex for a long time."

A few days later we met again to try to talk. Summery, sunlit people crowded the sidewalks as we walked down toward the Museum of Natural History.

"We just hit a bump," I explained. "That's all. It's not anything we can't . . ."

"What do you want? Tell me *that*! Do you know what Rilke said about criticism? You don't know that the back of the sun is blue. I was dancer and I despise men. You're not a spiritual person." It keeps going, a mad monologue that careers from one association to another, never letting you interrupt or pin it down.

"Just let me say one thing . . . ," I try.

She continues, a zigzagging maze of notions, clichés, nitwit new-age-isms, biblical quotes, repeated with emphatic satisfaction.

"Cast your bread upon the waters — *upon the waters*!" She thrusts her face toward mine, one hand raised in a grace note of perfect pitch: conductor of truth.

I keep attempting to break in. I want to calm the waters. She won't listen to me. I'm like a child that the waves will slaughter. To try to reason with her is futile, a madness to meet her madness, to be lost together in the wilderness of herself. I catch her arm as she turns away from me; she pulls loose with wild violence. People on the sidewalk step around us. I grab her again, insistent that she listen.

"Please, let me talk for one minute," I say.

"Let go of my arm! I'll call the police!" she screams.

She walks away. I throw the bottle of water I'm carrying down onto the sidewalk; it ricochets with a loud thud into a parked car. Everyone turns around except Irina, who moves swiftly down the street. It's all over in a second, vanishing into the city air. I cross the street and sit on a bench beside the park. At the light, Irina stands in a crowd of people. She looks awkward, as if her clothes don't fit. Her face is stunned, bewildered. I watch her without her knowing it as she crosses to the bus stop. Her eyes look broken. I go over and put my arms around her shoulders and lead her back to the bench like a sleepwalker. She permits it. The righteous march is over for the moment. Soft disks of light waver like water on the ground in the shade of overhanging leaves. All arbitration is brittle, a small boy's fight to prove that not to adore him was a terrible error in the logic of the world. The sense of my own pain, which I have always so efficiently transposed to a structure of justice, is suddenly dislocated in a newly formed landscape. Beyond any notion of right or wrong, like a mountain coming apart into its brushstrokes, there is only the overwhelming presence of her feelings, the hurt that harms her. I kiss her unresponsive mouth again and again, saying I love you I love you I love you I love you I love you I love you I love you. And then she is kissing me back, with an almost imperceptible movement of her lips, like dying words.

We walked north along the edge of the park. We'd done what we had never done. The conflict, if not solved, had been set behind us. She had stayed. We'd survived. She was even tentatively proud of having acquired a new strength in surmounting grown-up difficulties. We stopped at a deli and picked up a few things. I felt it. She said, "Don't worry, everything is fine. We're back together. I love you. I'm just tired and want to sleep at home tonight." The next day she had changed. She refused to meet me anymore.

Did she, on these occasions, revert to a position that represented her truest desires, or was it just the opposite: were her truest desires the casualties of a repeated collapse? Tell me, H.D.

I called, wrote her letters and e-mails, without response. I finished the translation of "No Name." It was a curious poem for Irina to have chosen, coming when it did. Her unconscious mind was like a third guest at the table — I was accustomed to its glove-handed felicities. In the translations I speak, as it were, through Pasternak's voice to address an English reader; but with ventriloquial eloquence, in this poem, Pasternak speaks through my voice and addresses *Irina*.

No Name

Touch-me-not, coldly demure,
now you're all fire, all aflame.
Let me lock your beauty
in the dark tower of a poem.

Look how the fiery peel
of the lampshade transforms
the corner of the wall, the windowsill,
our shadows and our forms.

You sit cross-legged, alone
on an ottoman. In the light,
in the dark, either one,
going on in your childish spite.

Abstracted, you string beads
that scatter onto your dress.
You are much too sad,
your conversation ingenuous.

The word "love" is banal —
you're right. For you, I'll find a new
name for it. I'll change it all,
the words, the world too.

How can your depressed glance impart
the ore deposit of the feelings you had,
the secretly glowing layers of your heart?
Why do you look so sad?

The poem literally says things we had said to each other. I made up a stanza, which I thought of adding to the end of it.

Do you recognize yourself in this,
wide hips arching up from the bed?
The starfish silhouette of a kiss
burns like a candle in my head.

But by then she had taken herself beyond my reach. No games, no door left open the tiniest crack. Sweet nothings with their mawkish assumption of a common ground faced a withering intolerance.

Buying candles was one of the few ways she openly acknowledged our lovemaking. I lit candles her breath had last blown out — pale breasts falling forward into the sudden dark.

I circled around the same points, constructing in my mind over and over an architecture of the problems that separated us. It turned into an obsessive, sleepless enterprise. I'd wake up at four in the morning and, unable to go back to sleep, masturbate — not the curled shell of an embrace, but keening, sexual despair, a convulsion around her absence. I tried to work. I visited friends in the country. At a party in Tribeca, I ran into a woman I'd known casually for a couple of years, a journalist who had inherited a great deal of money and was living in Connecticut. She invited me up for the weekend. Blond, with the face of a debutante, she was in her early forties and had recently ended a relationship with a well-known photographer. "I'm functionally illiterate," she said, "even though I minored in English at Sarah Lawrence." She spoke of herself in the third person. "Miss Liddy didn't study the way she should have." The house was low and horizontal; its generous rooms and wide, glassed-in terrace faced the Sound. With her easy, open-ended manner, what might have been a pleasant and mature encounter served only to heighten my abject sense of loneliness. The clichés in her speech got on my nerves, its bland rhetoric. The train back to the city was crowded with suntanned teenagers and dozing couples. When we lose each other we lose the best of each other. In Irina's case this was true with special poignance. It was easy to separate her from what she was not and to think only of what she might be. Not just memory but the medium of thought, its compass of order, creates an Irina in its own image. That's the one you lose.

In a small Key West rental, decorated with brightly colored Haitian paintings, I sat looking at the phone I'd picked up and put down. Palms rattled against the porch in the night wind. A waste of jasmine and salt blew through the house. On my first trip to Key West I was nineteen. I climbed an outdoor stairway, latticework and seagrape leaves patterning the sunlight, to the second floor of a house where a girl, a young artist, lived. The interior was cool and dark against the scorching heat, with aluminum lawn furniture in the rooms. Out the open door you could see the ocean over the tops of shiny roofs and the carmine blossoms of poinciana trees.

Key West echoed the squalor and romance of Galveston, but with the appeal of an artifice, prettier, bluer. This time I'd spent two weeks on the island unable to rouse myself. The traffic was depressing, the spreading encroachment of tropical kitsch. Earlier in the evening, at a bar built out over the water, I sat under clear stars waiting with nervous impatience to finish my drink.

I picked up the phone again. My hand shook. Then her voice was on the line, racing in its blunt lyrical lack of articles from one thing to another. I can't remember what she said. It was like listening to gears slip, clichés and platitudes skirting, speeding, turning up the glint of a relevant thread and then spiraling off into hints, inferences, vergings. I listened to the physical presence of her voice in the same way one beholds a photograph. It didn't matter what she said. With a sort of second attention, I followed its formal patterns — the skittish rush from one assertion to another to prevent an intervening comment. "They want me to read, I don't know, they Russians, we all slept on the floor in sleeping bags." (No breath.) "The soul arrives by express, you know, federal express?" Or the sudden need to trump the conversation — "You'll never know!" inflicted like a silky taunt, and then repeated as a simple fact: "You'll never know."

Two nights later, back in New York, I met her at the fountain at Lincoln Center. As she crossed the plaza I could see a wave of self-consciousness pass over her, a small falter in her stride, which galloped with stylish insouciance, one foot landing exactly in front of the other, along a straight line. Watching her approach, I felt — in a way that included the garish posturing of her life — how brave she was.

"Hello," she said.

"Do you know what negative ions do?" I asked.

"No, I don't," she said.

"They make you happy. Let's sit here by the fountain for a while."

And there she was. Specimen of the tribe of *pieridae*, perched on the mirror's edge.

Expressed as trajectories that begin in mutual, remote obliv-
ion — to meet in the dark grid of the world — our lives encounter, in the intersections they light up, their own novel absolutes.
Beyond my hopes or even the stridency of my desires — like
an event accidentally glimpsed that took in, at the same time,
its own impossibility — somehow, in a remarkable integration
that involved age difference, talent, nations, insanity, and lit-
erature, I knew, wholly and selflessly knew, that, *for this girl*,
I was the one. It wasn't solipsistic not to put it the other way
around: I was finished; she was alive. It was in fact precisely
because the thought presented itself in such immodest terms
that it possessed the impartiality of a truth. I knew the extent
of Irina's problems and measured her soul against them; I
was a poet, capable of recognizing the value of her talent, its
gleaming, fugitive strengths; I wanted her survival to hinge
not on self-debasement but on the discovery, in the correla-
tion of poetry and love, of her own powers. Somebody else
will do it differently. It'll be called destiny. But there's always
one person who vanishes with the life we didn't live — a life
made vivid by being no longer possible. I'm a fiction in its
value, not an ego. The whole thing is projected on the stars.

For Irina, agreed-upon meanings had no permanence. Being
with her entailed a continual redefining of the terms that
made being with her possible — not minor adjustments, but a
rigorous struggle carried out day after day against our immi-
nent dissolution. "One of us has to remain sane," she said, and
urged me to be patient. Yet it was Irina herself who conspired
against our success. To prove the insufficiency of love, she
searched tenaciously for a way out, running like a figure in a
movie, down the black-and-white corridors of her fears.

From Lincoln Center we walked across Broadway to the Brasserie Americaine, and ordered a glass of wine. We'd sat here dozens of times, Irina nibbling on tuna tartar and slivers of French bread. Against the dark wood of the high-backed booth, her face was radiant. In her speech, themes and combinations of themes followed one another in their usual jumble, but there was also a tentative new distance in her thought. Irina rarely expressed anything directly; she spoke with an excited agitation that moved from this to that, leaving phosphorescent allusions in its wake. She'd get lost in the details of her own stories. "I was in a hotel in Moscow. I was sixteen. A girlfriend and I promised this man that one of us would spend night with him if he got us case of fruit. My girlfriend did it. But in the morning when I came back to get her, the man said he didn't like her and that now I had to stay. There were no cops. He could just do whatever he wanted. And we had his fruit — you know, pomegranates? I loved fruit more than anything on earth. They come from south, around Black Sea. You open them and they have hundreds of tiny pink seeds. They like little jewels. I went to Black Sea when I was sixteen, with first Mafia guy. Nobody could bother you when you were girlfriend. His name was Vladimir. I was attracted to the power — you know? I was asleep in hotel, and an associate of his came and saw me. He offered Vladimir Rolex watch — you know, they even expensive here — to leave him alone with me for hour. I was so happy that Vladimir didn't sell me."

"But what happened with the other guy?"

"Who?"

"The guy in the hotel, with the pomegranates."

"Oh, nothing. I got away."

In the mosaic of her conversations, a vague moral uncertainty exists, a blur of running from unnamed consequences; the simplest human misdemeanors bear a subterranean weight. You want to stop her, hold her in your arms, and swing the heavy curtains back: See — it's O.K.

Tonight, even with all the indirection of her speech, a single concept began to emerge. It was, in effect, that the fear of loss paralyzes us, and because of it, we lose the things we want most. Irina lived in a web of blind actions and solo flight. This was different; it was an expression of self-knowledge, a rational perception forged out of her own head and heart and presented like a fragile contribution to potential happiness. It wasn't formed as a complete statement; it was gestured toward, approached in feints, elliptical passes, but it kept coming with a singular determination. "Let's say we have these apprehensions, doubts — you know, fears, sort of . . . that preehaps, I don't know, I mean, you want this to be, but, when comes to it, instead of trying, you do nothing — and then, lose it. Because — you know — you're afraid." She folded her arms in front of her, resting on her elbows. The waiters snaked through the tables outside our booth as the restaurant began to fill up with an after-theater crowd. In a calm, dusky voice, she said, "I wish I could touch you. I wish I could reach across the table and touch your hand."

As soon as the train left the city, climbing up into the light, the sky darkened and it started to storm. We took it as a good sign. Heavy rain fell evenly over a field of cattails. At the beach the first hotel we tried was full. The young woman working at the desk found us another hotel; then, like an act in a dream, walked out into the rain, wading in white sandals across the street through ankle-deep water to her car, and drove us there. From our room on the second floor we could see the slate-colored waves wrinkling in the wind. The next day was brilliant with sky-washed clarity. New understandings were in place. The first night there, when we made love, Irina whispered: "Now, this is really the beginning of something."

Back in New York, the red Russian-English dictionary was produced after dinner. It had the presence of a rare icon. The same wine, same blue ashtray filling up with her long, half-smoked cigarettes. We completed a first draft of "My Sister Life," and I read her a finished version of "Moochkop," a Pasternak poem we had worked on before.

Moochkop

Soul-stifled, the distance tobacco
colored — sort of — like thoughts.
The mills have a fishing village look:
weathered nets and boats.

Windmills numb in the village,
sails in still air,
everything is filled with fierce anguish,
impatience, despair.

Here an hour skips like a stone.
It ricochets over the shallows.
Alas, it doesn't sink, no,
it's still there, thought-like, brown.

Will I see her again? Certainly!
An hour till the train —
an hour embraced by apathy,
pitch-dark, imperiled, marine.

"Wow!" she said. "It's better than original!"
She leaned across the table giggling and pushed her lips against mine, swiveling her head from side to side in a little fanfare of passion.
"Really! It's great!"
We stayed up talking and watched the last half of *The White*

Sheik on TV. She was giddy and sweet, in a wonderful mood when we went to bed.

In the morning after Irina went home, I looked for the dictionary; it wasn't there.

"I'm not feeling very well."

This was code. It meant the psychic tide had changed. Her eyes wouldn't meet mine. Her mood disavowed any meaningful connection between us. Each time it happened — even though I knew it was inevitable — I was caught off guard. Recurring pain leaves a weak imprint upon memory; the defeating awareness of its repetition returns with each onset.

It was her birthday. She was wearing a gray-blue dress of sheer layers, with a delicate cape.

"You look great," I said.

"This?" she said, flicking her fingernails against her shoulder, with a weak, evaporating smile.

We were sitting at one of the front tables in Elio's.

I touched her glass with mine.

"This is two years in a row."

"Is it?" she said, coldly.

I could feel within myself the familiar descent, the poison entering the heart. I struggled to resist it and, like a child, despised myself for being unable to do so. The silence built up.

The restaurant was owned by a woman I knew. I had mentioned it once to Irina as a place where celebrities and the literary elite hung out. When we talked about her birthday, she suggested we go there. "What about that Elio's? We could do that — you know — just for fun."

"I've been here before," she said.

"Do you like it?"

A mask of ennui.

In one corner, there were groupings of framed book jackets on the wall. One of mine had been included — something the owner had done in part because we knew each other and in part because of an attractive cover drawing by James McGarrell.

I pointed it out to Irina. She at first refused to look, and then unobtrusively turned her head in its direction and turned back.

"Oh," she said.

"I should have let you spot it on your own," I said.

"But you didn't," she said.

The need to win her was a syndrome; I could only sink deeper, commit greater inanities. We ate in silence. The restaurant had been the wrong choice. In its East Side establishment aura, I felt like a caricature, an old man sitting with a bag of presents beside a bored glamour-girl.

"Where would you rather be?" I asked.

"Nowhere. What do you mean?"

"Maybe you'd be happier if you were with someone your own age."

"Maybe. We don't know," she said flatly. Then added, with a note of conciliation, "Age is not issue — you know that."

The restaurant was filled with people returning to the city, from the Hamptons, from Turks and Caicos, with tan animated faces.

"There are three things," Irina said. "Intimacy, love, and sex. I can't have all three at same time. One of them falls out. I can have intimacy and love, but not sex. Or I can have sex and intimacy, but not love."

"What about love and sex?" I asked.

"No, I can't have that," she said.

"Who told you this?"

"I figured out by myself."

An intimation, a glimpse of the backlit structure of regret passed through my mind. I could feel it, like a shell around me — as if the dream of being together or not being together was only a constant we conform to, and that beyond it lay the adulthood of love, the grail of maturity.

I gazed at the sheen of softly lit oak walls.

"No one knows what goes on between us," she said.

My dear Zaichik,
I can't express . . . how much you touched my heart smiled. It really did, or you did, we did . . .

Thank you so much. I probably haven't deserve having it all.

Sorry about last night. I crushed into pieces as soon as I reach the bed.
Love,
Irina

A day or so later, we met at the Metropolitan Museum, Irina arriving, as usual, half an hour late. I looked for, as she approached, a sign that would dispel, with a breath of relief, the foreboding suspense of what her state of mind would be. As she came up the steps her gaze turned away.

"Am I late?" she asked, her voice flat and cold.

"You're fine," I said.

An agitation played over her features, her evasive eyes.

"It's a beautiful day. We could do something outside if you want," I said.

"Well, we came to look at art," she stated curtly, as if it were an obligation that had to be discharged.

Inside the museum, we wandered around for a while, Irina uncommunicative. Her moods served notice. We walked up the wide stone staircase, untouching.

On the second floor, by standing at a particular place in one of the renaissance galleries, it was possible to line up the door-ways of several connecting rooms, creating a vantage point of unexpected distance; through doorframe upon doorframe upon doorframe, one could see, perfectly centered, a city block away, Rembrandt's *Self Portrait*.

"It's a nice thing to know about — don't you think?" I said.

A Russian shrug.

When she was like this, it was futile to ask what was wrong; she didn't know. And to found a discussion on what she might or might not say would lead only to further confusion. She would never look, even in a stable mood, if I pointed to something. I'd forget about this trait until it happened again, in the street, the subway, the park, an egret lifting off the lake. It was an act of militancy, rooted somewhere in her defenses, that turned itself into an exasperating farce.

She stopped in front of the Vermeer painting, *A Woman Asleep*. Our silence peered in at the young woman seated at a table with her head propped up on her hand.

"This is that Vermeer guy again," Irina said.

The plainness of the figure, so openly exposed, was almost a portrait of the opposite of Irina. As the label explained, a housemaid is dreaming of romance, symbolized by the Cupid's mask in a painting on the wall above her head. A further consequence, it occurred to me as we stood there, of depicting the subject asleep was that it made visible to the viewer her mind. The room she is in evokes the dream-disorder of love, a bottle overturned, a chair out of place and facing away from her, an opulent rug bunched up on the table — while through a half-open door, an empty room contains a calm geometry of forms.

We made our way back downstairs. As we were leaving Irina said, "I had a lot of past lives. I was sometimes man, sometimes woman. You don't believe these things, but they true. One — maybe two times more — they told me this — then I don't have to come back to world."

She addressed me as if I were a stranger, without any knowledge of her life or who she was. It had the affront of a psychotic act. I knew, to some extent, the etiology of these incidents. Like her recurring fixations on spiritual experiences or purity, it was a kind of diaphanous busywork at the level of her soul. But when it happened I couldn't avoid being affected by it. My heart sank, almost with the first word. That I knew, or thought I knew, was only a way of looking back.

Certain ideas reappeared, depending on which of her friends she was last with. Whenever she came from seeing Grigory, she sounded like a bad Russian version of Henry Miller. "This painter friend of mine is going to help me with connections — what difference does it make what you do in this shitty America?"

"Grigory?"

"Well, uh, yes . . . that happens to be his name. He's Russian, an artist," she said.

Grigory was one of the few people she saw on a regular basis. They'd had a brief affair three or four years earlier, and had remained friends. I once alluded to him as someone she had loved.

"I never loved Grigory," she stated flatly.

"You slept with him," I said.

"Just for fun," she replied.

Whenever she referred to new-age things, it meant she'd been talking to Otto, her "opera singer friend." The sole subject of Irina's conversations was Irina. She unfolded herself to everyone, like a board game where players were invited to entertain themselves by advancing the curious pieces of her self-seeking. She and I talked almost exclusively about her too; the difference was that we did it in a way that was tied to writing, so that the measure she took of herself was testable in the real world.

We sat outside on the small ledge at the front of the museum.

Irina lit a cigarette with a gold Dunhill lighter, staring off into space. I tried to think of something to say. These were episodes that mimed her loss; she disappeared from me, beyond my reach. To remain objective about what was happening was undermined by the impetuous and panicky longing to have her back.

"What do you think would be a more astonishing event," I asked, "to have painted the painting *A Woman Asleep* or to have been her in some past life?"

"You don't know about these things."

"So much time and effort is devoted to helping you try to think straight . . ."

"Don't holler," she said, glancing furtively around her.

"I'm not hollering," I said, in a frustrated whisper.

She got up and walked away. Orange light from the low sun burnished the upper facades of apartment buildings across Fifth Avenue. The air was still, a calm presence invading the city. Irina picked her way down the stairs, past Asian girls clustered on the steps, their black straight hair. This was her reaction to all conflict — to "discontinue." It happened again and again. Nothing could ever be resolved in a dialogue; differences slowly turned to scar tissue. At the bottom of the stairs, she didn't glance back; her gait as she walked past the fountain through the brightly colored mass of people was slow, resigned to itself, the sole tactic she possessed. *Let her go.* I watched her diminish as she wandered down the museum plaza toward Seventy-ninth Street. For a moment, I lost her in the crowd; then I saw her sit down on a bench, an almost indistinguishable figure in the distance. I was unable to move. *Let her go.* My own sanity seemed to receive an infusion from the peaceful detachment of the afternoon. Glittering conversations, lovers on the steps, quiet lives alone. Being with her was unbearable. Everything was layered in betrayals, so that jealousy became the normal response, a kind of spirit agony, permanently endured. I was worn out with it. *Let her go.* Like a process of working from one language to another, I watched her, too far away to do anything but torture myself with the idea that she had by now perhaps begun to seduce the stranger she sat down beside.

And yet, in Irina's case, betrayal itself was not fully responsible. I knew that I was shamefully at fault, reading into her struggles the tiresome spook of rejection (projected tellingly upon the isolate, the exception, the aberrant, instead of the whole). In the balance between us, sense and absurdity danced in my reason. But my depths could be scrutinized. I wanted her in my life. I was aware that nothing could be changed or overcome without first accepting Irina exactly as she was. I started down the block and caught up with her as she was crossing Seventy-ninth Street.

"I'm sorry," I said.

The Fifth Avenue bus pulled up beside us and she started to get on it.

"Where are you going?" I asked.

She looked at me and then turned away.

"Can I go with you?"

"It's free country."

Our being together, even though it proceeded day after day and except for a brief interruption had continued for more than a year, was normally treated by Irina as an undefined alliance. If I made a reference to myself as her boyfriend, her reaction was to dispute it as presumptuous. These were things wound into her nature and intended to some extent to be ignored. "You know I say things like this — why do you pay attention to me?" Yet it was an everyday threat, running like a lit fuse along the edge of each moment, that grace would be abruptly revoked. "Anyone can say 'Je t'aime' — it means nothing." Believing it to be a banality further forced the miracle of its proof. But in her denial was also a condemnation of the deceit and betrayal registered in the figures of language. With an honesty-beyond-hope, she scorched the earth of its speech. Talk of commitment, like all abstraction, was empty and imprecise. We had made promises, declarations, but always they were little more than mood decor, swept off the night table by a bare arm.

"If we both said to each other and meant it, 'I love you and want to be with you *no matter what*,' it would be a way of acknowledging that difficulties are going to happen but that we don't intend to be defeated by them," I said.

Throngs of young people spilled in and out of the bars we passed, absorbing carelessly lessons of similar import. Irina was tired but attentive.

"Is it possible for you to say that?" I asked.

"Yes," she said.

"Do it."

"I love you and want to be with you."

"No matter what?"

"No matter what."

Ever since I returned from Florida and we got back together, she'd been unable to enter into the trust of what our lives had been before. She stood like an animal at the edge of the woods. She avoided sleeping with me unless we went out of town. To make love in the city where we lived was not an "escapage"; it meant more. Whatever calculus proved the distinction, a new gravity had been added, revealed if in no other way than by the boundaries intended to contain it — and the need to escape.

"Do you mean what you're saying?" I asked.

"Yes," she said.

"Say it again."

She looked directly into my eyes, her face lit by street glare.

"I want to be with you . . . no matter what."
"I love you," I said.
"I love you," she said.
"Please don't change this time," I said.
"I don't think I will," she said.

I sent her a one-word e-mail the next day: "Continuity." The following day, I sent the finished draft of Pasternak's famous poem "My Sister Life." In it a Russian train, like the incarnation of a lover, races from stop to stop across an endless landscape of spring. She didn't respond. I called her several times and got either her machine or no answer. A week went by like this. I knew what had happened, what had always happened.

Finally, from a pay phone, dodging her caller ID, I reached her. She sounded like a zombie when she said hello, and hung up as soon as she heard my voice. I called her back; she hung up again. I took a cab to her building and ran up the three flights of stairs to her apartment. The hope that something else could explain what had happened, a crisis separate from us, opened its own prongs of panic in my mind. I knocked on the door. There was no answer. I knocked again.

"Irina! Please talk to me. Are you all right?"

I stood waiting, looking down at the gray and black linoleum tiles, their galactic swirls spattered with green paint. There was no response. I tried to open the door, but it was locked. I banged on it with my fist.

"Irina! Talk to me! Please!"

Within the stillness of the building, I stood listening. The apartment was silent. I went back down the stairs. From a pay phone on the corner, I called her again. My glance passed over the abandoned mansion across the street, the night sky showing through its roof of domes, its roof of dreams. Her machine answered.

I said: "Please tell me what's wrong. I'm worried about you . . ."

She picked up the phone and started screaming.

"If you don't leave me alone, I'm going to call the police! I don't want to be with you anymore! I don't love you — I love somebody else! Good-bye!"

We are the counterstress that completes the measure. Our lives occupy both places — their own and the empty steppe — a moment after the rhyme tolls. In the quiet hour, the train's passage erupts into the darkness. Then the noise recedes, a faint, metallic murmur, delicate as a flower. It seems to come from right beside you in the air.

epilogue

With Irina nothing could be counted on, not even the worst. Like her clothes or the way she tasted ("I taste like roses"), it was a quality that had become, in my perceptions, simply one more evocation of her presence. But despite my hopes, we didn't get back together. Apparently there wasn't anyone else in her life. We met for dinner a few times, and walked back along the edge of the park, our arms around each other. She had once said, six months ago, "If we lose, it's because Elvira has won." I believed it, but was also aware that it altered nothing, like the naming of Elvira in the first place. This was love, its broken armature. The reasons behind it were irrelevant. Toward the end, nothing could be discussed between us. Any attempt hit the blades of her defenses. Because of course everything had been said a thousand times. We were finished; even I knew it.

The Pasternak translations had been left in various stages of incompleteness. After a while I decided to try to finish them by myself — not as a potential contribution to the body of Pasternak's work in English, but because Irina's voice ran through them, a bright strand, in a braid with my own. Our contact ended. The storm has moved out to sea. I'm turning other pages. But Irina's own poems — the ones she showed me when we first met, and the others she wrote while we were together — ghost through my mind. This book, on one level, is an apotheosis of their absence, as if the translation of Pasternak's verse were emblematic of something turbulent, harder and less knowable that shared in its example. They were love poems in the most literal sense: the collaborative process of their making was, except as the work of lives deeply bound together, inconceivable. In a way, they belong to neither of us anymore.

Six months after we broke up, I received a package from Irina. The sight of her handwriting, her name in the return address, affected me with lightheaded anticipation and dread. I sat down and opened the package with a sense of ceremony. The room was dark, except for a reading lamp on my desk. She had sent one of her collages. It was deftly made, with poetic images. A cutout figure of the Mona Lisa was pasted onto the middle of the page. Above it, as if sprouting out of the top of her head, was a pair of feathery angel's wings. The open wings, and the folded hands of the Mona Lisa, produced a formal correspondence that was reinforced by a second pair of hands reaching up from the bottom of the composition. A dragonfly paused between them in midflight, beside an actual feather, gray with white markings on its tip. But the most riveting feature, which served as a ground for the whole collage, was the lead-sheet of a song from my play. In the song, a female character tells her ex-husband that she has never stopped loving him, taking a courageous and disarming first step toward the possibility of reconciliation. With a rush of emotion, I let my eyes run over the surface of the collage. I looked at it for a long time, hardly knowing what I thought; or rather, knowing exactly what I thought, but uncertain of how to express or act upon it. Finally I decided to try to make something to send to her in return. Making things for each other was a form of communication. But for me it was also a willful confounding of the person and the thing; it had Galatea's being, touched and coaxed eagerly to life.

During the next few days I wrote a short play, whose simple conceit was that its characters personified the conflicting thoughts and feelings that receiving the collage had caused in me. The primary characters in the play were famous Russian authors, which gave to the act of writing it a sense of silliness, an intimate leeway, in which serious things were said.

The play begins with Chekhov stepping out of the shadows near a bookcase in my apartment. I am a character in the drama and sit at my desk looking at the collage. He asks me what it is. When I tell him that Irina sent it, his response is immediate and unequivocal: he urges me to throw it away. I make an effort to soften his position, but he is adamant. "I know her, completely know her, if only through your despair." He refuses even to glance at the collage. When I tell him how good it is and begin to describe it, he adjures me to stop. From the same shadows, Gogol enters and says that, on the contrary, I should be permitted to describe the collage. "One can often discover just how important or unimportant a person is by describing what they do. The threads get bare quick enough. She may only be a minor figure after all." I then resume my description, with Chekhov interjecting occasional sarcastic comments. "*The Mona Lisa*? Please!"

Along one side of the collage Irina had written a line in gray ink — a statement signed with her initials. I could feel the intention of her mind, its push against the syntax. In the play, describing the collage to Chekhov, I read the statement aloud: "*If dreams wouldn't exist, we wouldn't know the difference.*" A long pause follows. In an incredulous tone, Chekhov says, "*What?*" There is a second pause, and Gogol echoes, "*What?*" Then the boffo pause — the third voice — "*What?*" as Dostoevsky enters. The three men discuss the statement and conclude that it is nonsense. "Our Russian women," Gogol says, "slip a little this way and that way." Chekhov again advises me to throw the collage in the garbage. "You are an idiot if you don't."

Writing the play, late at night and alone, I relish its license, the freedom to express through a chorus of voices positions I know to be valid. At the same time I watch the center drift. As the action continues I try to offer a defense of Irina's statement, claiming that the only problem is that it's unfinished, and that what she means is that if dreams didn't exist, we couldn't know the difference between "something" and "something else" — the missing x and y in her argument — and that had they been included, her statement would have the logic of a proof. At this point, Pasternak enters in a white suit and stands leaning against the doorframe of my room. "That is what you always do," he says. "You transform her incoherence into shiny new words. I agree with my comrades; enough is enough. Walk away from it." The others nod in agreement, except for Dostoevsky, who quietly broods. (Mitya's redeeming, unstoppable, operatic pursuit of Grushenka in *The Brothers Karamazov* had been a part of our cosmology.) When Dostoevsky finally speaks, he says, "It's not a question of coherence; it's a question of love. I think he should keep the collage, hang it on his wall, and hope it's an overture, an opening. Incoherence means nothing. Love is the highest stake — you either refuse to gamble or you risk everything."

Suddenly, another character enters from the shadows, a beautiful and ethereal woman. She explains that she is the Spirit of My Future Love. "You'll meet me. I'm on the subway, in the park, I'm walking toward you on the street," she says. "Love is a gamble, yes, but the odds don't have to be stacked so utterly against you. I'm real. I exist somewhere on the other side of this moment. We will meet, hold hands, kiss a thousand kisses. *We* will prevail." Her fingers touch my face. I stand mesmerized by her. "But no one," I remark, "can ever be quite as perfect as you are." She answers, "How can you be sure? Wait until you meet me; I might be more wonderful than you can imagine."

That song.

"Tell me . . ." I say.

"Yes . . . ?"

I hold up the collage.

"Is it possible . . . is there any possibility . . . that *you* sent me this?"

"Is that what you want to gamble on?" Her voice is almost a whisper.

I place the collage against the wall again and stare at it.

"Yes, that's what I want. Is it possible?"

There is no reply. When I look up the room is empty. The shadows have surrendered their mysteries. The play ends with the collage sitting on my desk, in the glow of the lamp.

I mailed the play to Irina, and a few days later she called.

"Well . . . if you can, I would like see some paintings, or we could meet — you know — some place in daytime, and just talk. I have something to tell you."

We met uptown at a restaurant on the East Side. It was a cold March afternoon. The restaurant was almost empty, its white tablecloths and wicker chairs lit only by the outside light of gray sky, through the tall windows. The room was barn-like, with high ceilings and ocher walls decorated with frescoes of summery Italian beach scenes.

She walked in wearing a stylish winter coat, pale blue with dark felt on its collar, and stepped uncertainly around the sea of tables, tall, exotic, waving midway.

"Well, I thought I should have a pink balloon, so you know who I am," she said, laughing with the corners of her mouth turned down. She sat across from me. "Lately I've been into pink — you know, *pink*."

She ordered a glass of wine, quizzing the waiter for his recommendations and deciding on a Cabernet. When he brought it she said, "Is this heavy?"

"It's a full-bodied wine," he said.

"Oh . . . I better not . . . do you mind . . . ?"

"You want something else?" he asked.

"Well . . . what do you have that's light?"

"Maybe a . . . Chianti?"

"Yes, that's what I want!"

The waiter, a small, disoriented Ecuadorean, took the Cabernet away and returned with a new glass of wine. I thanked him. It was like slipping back, with seamless ease, into our lives.

"I'm very glad to see you," she said.

The apprehension and mixed feelings that surrounded her in my mind were dissolved like wayward hallucinations by her presence. In these first moments with Irina, I experienced the keen cessation of small, unslaked longings, fulfilled solely through the immediacy of her Persian eyes, the luster of her skin.

She began to tell me about her job. She was working backstage in the costume department for a big Broadway show.

"My boss is mean. She is black woman, who wears red sweater tied across her chest, like wounded soldier. I am only per diem — you know, per diem — the lowest people. They don't like me. But let me show you something."

She took a folder out of her bag and began to rummage through it.

"Oh, look!" she said, distracting herself. She took out several photocopies of old photographs. "I'm making collage for my parents — for anniversary. This is my father, and this is my mother — when they were first married."

Her father was sober-looking, handsome in a conventional way, her mother's face pleasant, but unremarkable.

"This is my brother," she said, pointing to a blurry image of a young man in uniform.

"Is this you?" I said, picking up another picture.

"Yes," she said.

I had never seen a photograph of her as a child.

"How old are you here?" I asked.

"Oh, three or four."

"This is before your brother began to . . ."

"Yes, before."

I stared with absorption at the image of a dark-haired, diminutive girl, sitting at a small table.

"Do you have another copy of this?" I asked.

"You can have it," she said.

She gathered up the others and put them back.

"This is what I wanted to show you," she said, handing me a photograph mounted on matboard of a nude woman, lying on her back, with Irina's face peering over her stomach.

"I'm making series of erotic images of women. That's what I'm finally discovering about myself," she said.

"Is this what you were going to tell me about?" I asked.

"No, I'm just showing you this. That's me," she said, pointing to herself. She put the photo back in her bag. Once or twice, during the time we had been together, she talked about sexual experiences she'd had with women, intimating that it was experimentation that belonged to the past.

"Does this mean you've decided to be interested in women?" I asked.

"No . . . I don't have woman lover right now," she said. And then added, "Men, women — it doesn't matter — I have no boundaries."

The light was fading in the windows. A few early diners had drifted into the restaurant. A busboy was setting out candles on the tables.

"What did you want to tell me about?" I asked.

"Maybe we should do it another time," she said. "We could eat oysters at Grand Central. I have to be at work by six-thirty."

"No, tell me now — it's why we met. You've got plenty of time," I said.

She glanced around the restaurant.

"Well . . . O.K.," she said.

She leaned forward on one elbow.

"I can't speak loud," she said, looking up at me, "and nei-ther can you."

"No one can hear us," I said.

"Well . . . you know how I get along with gays. They a big part of the theater, I work with them all the time. They love me for some reason. Maybe because I'm Russian, or because fashion, or because I'm crazy. Who knows? Anyway, I was shopping for vegetables at store on Upper West Side — you know, on Broadway — and this guy was there, he was buying broccoli or something and talking to me. So, we had coffee and started meeting, you know, he has teaching job at CUNY, and I would go up to see him. The cleaning ladies would be in the hall — can you imagine! — and we're right there. He's bisexual."

"You were making love?" I said.

"Not really going inside — well, maybe a couple of times — but you know kissing," she said.

Her arm lay across the table in front of her, the palm of her hand facing up, her wrist. She had on a thin, opal-green sweater.

"We would go to gay bars, you know, and he would pick up somebody. They usually scared of me. He has beautiful penis. When we first met he gave me photograph of himself — you know, *up* — taken behind a net veil."

The same voice, the same hiatus-laced candor, had talked about her poems at midnight, confided her dreams. Its timbre vibrated in membranes of inchoate sense.

"When did you meet him?" I asked.

"Oh, three, four months ago — just let me tell you. So, at one point he showed me his belt. He has a belt — you under-stand? He taught me how to put it on. So, I did," she said.

"What do you mean — for a *dildo*?" I asked.

"Yes," she said. "I wore it."

Her face was very close to mine, the color of her hair nearly black, with the ends frosted gold.

"You fucked him in the ass?" I said.

"Yes. Belt fits very tightly around you. So then," she giggled, "I went down to that lesbian store in Village and bought one of my own. You can boil it — you know, for germs. I got three sizes — they have lots different kinds — but he only likes big one."

Some people came in and were seated at a nearby table. Irina leaned closer to me to finish what she had to say. In the mirror at the end of the room I could see the two of us, small in the distance, our lives lived by strangers.

"He told me that for first time he felt like a woman," she said. "Because I can do — you know — to him exactly what I would want being done to me."

She sat back in her chair, a small nervous grin disappearing as her face mimed a tactful solemnity.

"It took a lot of courage to tell you this," she said.

"Why *did* you tell me?" I asked.

"I wanted you to know this hidden side of who I am," she said.

The waiter came over to see if we wanted another drink. Irina looked at her watch.

"I wish I could stay," she said solicitously. "I have to brush teeth. If they smell this wine, they'll fire me. I can't be late. I've stopped being late," she said.

I helped her on with her coat.

"We can get together soon," she said, "next week maybe — if you want to." At the door she turned, wiggled her fingers in the air, and disappeared.

I walked across the park to the West Side, past the Great Lawn with its view of midtown skyscrapers, luminous in the distance. I was at once calm and reeling with a flux of thoughts and fragmented images. A part of my mind assembled, almost as she spoke, not a rationale for her behavior, but an understanding of the sense it made in Irina's life. I felt the logic of it with the infallible cognition of jealousy, but without its will to disbelieve. The role-playing, the pseudo-freedoms and absence of emotional demands, the life-habit of transposing self-degradation and tenderness were all there. Plus, who was I to say that a gay ethic, shaped by mordant realism, would not be the instrument of a new hegemony? The ground became a blur as I walked. I didn't disapprove of her. The welling desolation I experienced was not because she had traveled beyond my reach to a newfound dimension in herself, but because I understood, more than ever before, that for all her iridescent movement in the world, the distance that separated us would remain unchanging.

On the subway I stood leaning against the doors at one end of the half-full car. I was crying. It occurred to me that a corollary truth, which I did not want to face, was that we were no farther apart now than we had ever been. I couldn't quite focus my mind. I had clearly expected something different. But the shock I encountered was not totally due to the things she told me. For a long time I had conceived of Irina's limitations in terms of what stood between us and finally made things impossible. Because they were so painfully real, it had been a logical step and one that Irina, while we were together, had corroborated. "I just need to get few things straightened out in my mind — then, we will be happy." What I realized now was that her problems meant something entirely different in the world. They were not decipherable as one half of an equation that exhibited the solipsistic proof of why I was not loved. Right or wrong, her life was running on its own tack, unrelated to mine. I could no longer define through its condition my own contingent hopes. The relation between the two had vanished. She was separate, free.

The image hung in my mind, of Irina leaning forward on her elbows, her face inches from mine, in the bleached yellow of the restaurant. Her physical presence was intense, bathed with a disavowal of all history. I tried to imagine myself, like Hemingway in *The Garden of Eden*, accepting as a part of the dark matter of the universe an unendurable situation. The train clattered into the next station. On the platform commuters stopped their ears against the screech of metal. A young Asian woman got on the train and sat down across from me. Opening a book with a green and white patterned cover, she read it from back to front, like a person in a mirror.

I felt defeated, reduced to a dead level of inevitability. I'd known all along how hard it would be for Irina to have a serious relationship with anyone. The primary theme in our lives had been that we would someday achieve it. She'd bring it up with child-like excitement, the bright abstraction of the idea. I believed in the future. I understood it as an object of our mutual pursuit, foreshortened by kisses, by days and nights. Belief remains intact, like a scale of one's losses, in the meaning it has conferred on the past. In retrospect, to acknowledge that dildos, Cartier watches, and poems were for Irina little more than the interchangeable baubles of a fractured attention was to face the degree of my own distorted sense of our lives. I could feel in myself the corrosive error, branching backwards in time, depleting reality of what I thought had been otherwise. But it was not all an illusory past. We were together longer than she had been with anyone else, except for the Russian Mafia boss, when she was a teenager. She was tragic, fragile, deranged. In her mind the black shapes of sex and love separated like a breathed-on mobile. There had been undeniable moments, which were lost to her as much as to me.

In the final inventory nothing had counted, because nothing could.

I got off the subway and climbed the stairs to the street, looking up between buildings at the blue incandescence of dusk.

She is three and a half and sits at a child's table, in a room of rose-patterned wallpaper. A Plexiglas box of pencils and a few sheets of blank paper are arranged in front of her, beside a blond doll with outstretched legs. Another, smaller doll is held in both hands, pressed to her chest. Her hair is cut short in uneven bangs. She has on a round-collared, sleeveless dress. Arched with the angled break of bird wings, her eyebrows are dark and thick. Within the round heart-shape of her face, they seem incongruously adult. But her eyes are the eyes of a child, black with shining catchlights, the one turning in toward the other. The most arresting quality of her face is its expression. She stares up at a point above the camera — at the photographer. Her eyes convey a consenting participation; they are lit not by happiness but by a silent appeal to its potential occasion. Her mouth is compressed, flexing into a lopsided smile, constrained by the extra-dimpled stress of her chin and lower lip. Yet the delicate life of tensions in her face — enhanced by her grown-up eyebrows — is subdued by an unmistakable acquiescence, as if the world were measured against a resigned belief that the moment of happiness will not survive.

About two months after our meeting in the restaurant, I received an announcement in the mail from the Bowery Arts Club. On the front of the card was a picture of Irina wearing a lacy garter belt with tinted stockings and shiny black shoes. Her legs are crossed, her face turned haughtily away to one side. In white empty space she sits on a metal folding stool, leaning forward with her breasts, above the thin scallop of her bra, edged slightly together by the angle of her arms. It was a photograph from before I knew her, when she wore her hair long. Across the top of the card, in large bold type, was written IRINA MIROPO; at the bottom it said, POETRY STRIP. The copy on the other side of the card read:

Announcing:
IRINA MIROPO
Performing a Live Striptease
Reading Her Poem
RESURRECTION

Underneath this Irina had written, "You're Invited." I made a note on my calendar and kept the card on my desk for a few days. After a while I transferred it to a drawer, with the rest of her letters. As the date drew closer, the first unsettled days of spring turned warm. Forsythia bloomed in the park. In the end I didn't go, but I thought about it.

Printed in the United States
by Baker & Taylor Publisher Services